D0867984

TREASON

It Was The End Of Camelot...

But Not The End Of Valor

TOM SALVADOR

author**HOUSE**®

AuthorHouse™
1663 Liberty Drive
Bloomington, IN 47403
www.authorhouse.com
Phone: 1-800-839-8640

This book is a work of fiction. Names, characters, places and
incidents are products of the author's imagination or are
used fictitiously. Any resemblance to actual events at locales
or persons living or dead is entirely coincidental.

© 2011 Tom Salvador. All rights reserved.

No part of this book may be reproduced, stored in a retrieval system, or
transmitted by any means without the written permission of the author.

First published by AuthorHouse 3/11/2011

ISBN: 978-1-4520-9358-1 (sc)
ISBN: 978-1-4520-9359-8 (e)

Library of Congress Control Number: 2010916431

Printed in the United States of America
Any people depicted in stock imagery provided by Thinkstock are models,
and such images are being used for illustrative purposes only.
Certain stock imagery © Thinkstock.

This book is printed on acid-free paper.

Because of the dynamic nature of the Internet, any Web addresses or
links contained in this book may have changed since publication and
may no longer be valid. The views expressed in this work are solely those
of the author and do not necessarily reflect the views of the publisher,
and the publisher hereby disclaims any responsibility for them.

Edited by : TABulation PROse
Cover idea by : Tom Salvador
Cover created by : Damian Barker Graphic Design, Inc.

Books by Tom Salvador

The Midas Man
The Ring Master
Treason

Dedicated to My Love, My Wife,

Bernadette

In Loving Memory of

Joseph (Joe) Ostaseski, Jr.
&
William (Bill) Panagot

❧ ACKNOWLEDGMENTS ❧

I am forever grateful to be able to tap into the wisdom of special people. They gave me their time, time and again, and I cannot thank them enough. Every aspect of *Treason* was personally researched, including: a motor trip to the Southwest and the hands-on personal experience of my friends.

The following advisors are not responsible for the fictionalized content of this novel, nor have they had any input on how their information was used.

Spanish Interpreters:
    Mercedita O'Connor
    Rudy Sobers

Law Enforcement:
    Cindy L. Baldwin, Capt. (Commander, PA) –
    Investigation and Forensics
    Michael D'Arco, Sgt., M.P., USA/Police Officer, NJ(Ret)
    – Southwest Region

Jeffrey McGunnigle, Lt., NYPD(Ret) – On-the-job,
Weapons and NYC
Joseph Ostaseski, Jr., Chief of Police(Ret) – FBI
Shirley Wendler – NYPD Academy

Aeronautics:
Dr. Tim Goslee

Military:
Paul Flebotte, Col., USA(Ret)

A SPECIAL THANKS:
To the Congressional Medal of Honor Society and Museum
in Mount Pleasant, South Carolina, for permission to use
their image of the Medal of Honor.

✖ CHAPTER ONE ✖

The transfer from light of day to dusk is always more pronounced in a city than it is in the suburbs, and is especially true for a big city like New York. As the late September sun disappeared behind tall buildings, their shadows emitted a chill, long before darkness prevailed. It was a child's sundial – a signal to go home for dinner.

On 15th Street in lower Manhattan, the cockroaches, being lured by the garbage put out for the morning pick-up, were beginning their routine of crawling out to the sidewalk. Danny McCoy had found their homes in the wooden stairs and cracked concrete leading up to the apartments over the store fronts. The entire block, except for one place, had colonies, and Danny knew where every one was. This was his entertainment before returning to his new address.

Danny's stuttering increased with each change of school as he had to get past the taunts of his less than understanding classmates. *Why don't I stutter when I'm thinking?* He had no one to ask, but he did know the day it all began.

Six years ago, the worst day of his life; both of his parents were killed in an auto accident and there were no other living relatives, or any that would come forward – foster care began. He often looked for a safe place to cry. *I don't stutter when I cry, either.* Not being wanted, unloving foster parents, and unfriendly peers made being by himself the lesser of evils, and his first choice.

The sign said, "The Honor Boxing Club," and was the only building on the block that did not have cockroaches. Danny McCoy looked into the club through its open doorway. He heard one voice above all others, speaking with a *thick* Spanish accent.

"Throw *jour* punch and then bring it back. What *jou* find so hard about that? *Jou* going leave your glove out there, doing nothing? *Jou* see an opening, *jou* punch, then *jou* go back to defense. Punch, defense, punch, defense. Now, if *jou* see *jour* punch do some damage, then *jou* double up with *jour* punches; if he looks hurt, again, *jou* keep punching at different angles, but be careful." His voice rose. "He could be playing possum. *Jou* can tell by looking at his eyes; look deep into his eyes, they can tell *jou* how the fight is going. Punch, punch, punch, but always be ready to defend." Hector Lopez was speaking to his newest member Bobby Perkins. Perkins had heard of Hector's reputation with young fighters and was willing to take in his hard work ethic.

"Daddy!" Tito called out. Because of their adulation toward their father, both Tito, age sixteen and Mario, age fifteen, Hector's two sons, spent as much time as they could at the Club. And because of their constant calling out to him, the handlers, trainers, fighters and just about everyone else at the club took to calling Hector Lopez, "Pops" in place of "Daddy." He did not care for it, but he was overwhelmed by its use and learned to live with it.

"Daddy" Tito called again. "I see that skinny *white* kid every day at our door. Maybe he's a runaway?"

"Don't *jou* have something better to do then look out the door? Don't *jou* have homework or something?"

"My school had a teacher's conference today. No school and no homework."

"*Jou* and *jour* brother *jou* have quick mouths, but slow feet and hands. I know *jour* mother's happy about that." Marisol Lopez *was* happy that her two sons would not be following in her husband's footsteps. Hector agreed, but for different reasons. He felt that their skills fell short of being a professional fighter, and because of this, they could be seriously injured. He allowed them to help out at the club, as sons of the owner, but not as members.

Marisol was second generation Puerto Rican descent and had graduated from CCNY (City College of New York). She taught Kindergarten through sixth grade until she started having children. In Hector, as she often said, "I saw the goodness of his heart and the strength and fairness of his soul." Of course, as she would add, she was not put off by his chiseled features, superb physique and his confidence of not being intimidated by her looks or education.

Hector Lopez was drafted into the United States Army from his native land of Puerto Rico and trained as a medic. It was during the Vietnam War that he was awarded his nation's highest medal for bravery, The Congressional Medal of Honor. He never spoke about what he did to earn it, nor did he ever take any advantage of being a recipient. When he came out of the service, he moved to the United States and became a professional boxer. He met Marisol while traveling on the same subway train from The Bronx. She was on for three stops to a school where she taught, while he stayed on into Manhattan where he trained. They were an unlikely pair – he the macho street wise boxer, and she the sophisticated, well educated beauty. Along with her slim figure, dainty features, and her long flowing black hair, were her deep glistening brown eyes that seemed to take in everything around her. She disliked boxing and would not go to any of his matches. Not long after marrying and starting a family, Hector gave up fighting, but not boxing. He opened "The Honor Boxing Club." It was the only reference to his medal that he ever made. The name of the boxing club was never explained and most people did not know the true meaning of "Honor." Besides their two boys, Hector and Marisol also had a girl they named Maria, who was the same age as Danny McCoy.

❦ Chapter Two ❦

"Did *jou* do your roadwork this morning?" Hector asked of his newest fighter, Bobby Perkins.

"Yes, Pops, I did like you said, running and sprinting, running and sprinting."

Hector cringed; it was the first time Perkins used "Pops." He let it go.

"Good! Conditioning is the most important thing for a fighter. *Jou* can have a big punch or be the best boxer in the world, but if *jou* get winded real fast, then *jou* going to lose every time." Hector handed him a jumping rope.

"*Jou* know how to use this?"

Perkins took it from Hector's outstretched hand and proceeded to show off. Leaving little room for clearance, he jumped with his feet together, crossing them and moving them side to side, crossing his arms, and then swinging the rope to either side. Hector held up his hand and Perkins stopped.

"Good! *Jou* going to use this along with road work. When *jou* come here, *jou* will warm up for twenty or thirty minutes before we do our boxing drills. *Jou* will see your footwork improve along with your stamina. Jumping rope is not for showing off, it's for showing up to fight, fully prepared."

Hector noticed Perkins looking over his shoulder.

"Who's that skinny kid at the door?"

As Hector turned around, Danny left.

"I don't know who he is, but I tell *jou* this, I will find out. He's like a ghost that every one has seen but me."

"Well if he is one, he's a skinny white ghost," said Perkins.

"Tito!" Hector motioned for his son to come to him. "The next time *jou* see this *fantasma* (ghost), invite him in. If nothing else, we'll see if he's hungry"

Two hours later, at 7 p.m., Danny was back looking in through the doorway. Tito called to him, "Hi." Danny stared at him for several seconds, before darting off. Tito went to his father.

"There's something about that kid that's very sad. I got close enough to see his face and he looked like he was hurting. Not from an injury, he had like pain on his face. That's the best I can explain it."

Hector was proud of his son's heart. *Jou can't teach that, jou can't buy that,* he said to himself. "*Jou* can go home now and tell *jour* Mother I won't be too late tonight."

Home was a single family house in Queens. Tito would be taking the subway home.

❧ CHAPTER THREE ❧

On Saturday morning, as he did most Saturdays, Hector took both sons to the Club. He walked around the ring and watched Tito working the *focus mitts* with Bobby Perkins. As Tito moved the mitts around at different angles, Perkins, at the same time, worked on his slipping and sliding. Hector liked what he saw.

He has the talent and is not afraid of working, Hector observed. *He could be the real deal.* As Hector wandered toward the door, he thought his eyes caught a shape move to the side. Instead of going directly out the door, Hector stepped to the side and very slowly moved toward the center of the door and then out.

Danny was standing just outside and off to the left. Hector startled him and Danny started to run.

"Please don't run son, stay here a second."

Two words stopped Danny from going any further, *please* and *son*. It was not often that he heard *please*, and he had not been any one's *son* in a long time.

"Do *jou* like boxing?"

Danny nodded his head.

"My name is Hector, what is *jour* name?"

"D..D..Danny M..M..C..Coy"

"Come inside with me Danny and I'll show *jou* around."
What has somebody done to this kid? Who are his parents?

Hector placed his hand on Danny's shoulder to lead him
in and Danny recoiled. *Oh my god, this poor kid can't take
in kindness.*

With his outstretched hand he showed Danny the way
into the Club. He led him to a small card table where a split
open box of doughnuts sat on display. There was a gallon
of milk, a coffee maker, a stack of napkins, packets of sugar
and stacked cups. Hector took a doughnut from the box and
motioned for Danny to take one. He poured Danny a cup of
milk without asking.

"We have ones with jelly in them!"

"Jelly d..doughnuts." replied Danny. He took one.

*That's it Danny, nice and easy...calm down, you're among
friends.* Hector's mind was in overdrive.

"Where do *jou* live Danny?"

"I...I live in..in the whi..white building." He pointed in
its direction.

"Oh yes, that's a nice place."

"N..no it's not."

Hector sensed a broken home or worse. *Something's
wrong here.*

"Who do *jou* live with?"

"M..my f..foster parents."

"How old are you Danny?"

"I...I'm al..most th..thirteen."

Hector slid the box of doughnuts over to Danny. His thin
hand went into the box and found another jelly doughnut.

Hector poured a second cup of milk into his coffee cup. Danny's sugar crusted fingers wrapped around the cup and, it too, was quickly drained.

"Can *jou* stay awhile, Danny? I'll show *jou* around and maybe teach *jou* a little about boxing. *Jou* know, with the gloves?" Hector's eyebrows rose in exclamation. "*Jou* can go home or make a call from here to let *jour* foster parents know."

Danny nodded and his eyes grew wide. "N..no n..need to call. They're n..not home."

Hector knew he would be getting a *yes* answer about boxing. *All boys like boxing.* Hector's feelings regarding his foster parents were mixed and he did not know why. He was angry that social services would place Danny with people who let him run loose and at the same time there was *something* that he did not understand. It was that it did not make him *that* angry.

∾

It was pizza and coke for lunch. Danny had three slices and his face showed it. This time, his slender hands were full of tomato sauce.

Hector laughed as he showed him the way to the sink to wash up. Danny laughed too. *If he stays here, this kid is not going to stay skinny.*

After lunch Mario found his own youth boxing gloves and both he and Hector put them on Danny. He did not flinch as they touched his arm while fitting the gloves on. Hector took note of that.

Danny had the gloves on and held them out in front of him. They looked to be a little smaller than his head. The look of awe on Danny's face gave Hector a sensation of euphoria. Again, he was perplexed by these emotions.

❧ CHAPTER FOUR ❧

Every day after school, Danny came to the Club. Hector gave him odd jobs and he became Mario's helper. Hector kept an eye on his second son so that Danny did not go from helper to slave. *Mario is a good kid but doesn't have the big heart like his brother.*

As Hector was taking in the whole club as a panorama, he thought back to the circuses he went to as a child and all of the acts going on at the same time. *Not much different even down to replacing the elephant smells with human odors.*

Tito came up behind him.

"I guess we should thank Danny for the variety of *cuisine* being offered here lately." Tito raised his eyebrows awaiting a response.

Hector smiled. "At least *jour* school is teaching *jou* some twenty-five dollar words."

"I think he's getting fatter, Daddy."

"I think *jou* are right son. I think *jou* are right."

Danny had become part of the club and a routine had set in. He was present and accounted for every day and weekends. Tito would help with his homework, and Bobby Perkins would see that he got home safely. Hector, however, was the one constant in all aspects of Danny's life at the club. It was three weeks into his initial entry when a major change took place.

"Time to take you back home, Danny," said Perkins.

"This *is* my home Bobby."

Hector heard this and walked over to them. "How would *jou* like to come home to my house Danny and meet the rest of my family?"

Danny nodded his head. There was less nodding these days as the stuttering decreased.

∾

"Where does he go every day? Don't you care?" Kerry Hoey asked a question that she knew what the response would be.

"What the fuck do I care or YOU for that matter. We get the check every month and now we don't even have to feed him," said John Hoey.

Kerry's looks had departed long ago. Her once cute face had become puffy and her one time, body to die for, had depreciated into a bloated stomach and a blotchy skin condition. She wore her hair pulled back creating a harsh look to an already stark appearance. Borderline alcoholism and being married to John Hoey contributed to this condition. She believed that he did not have an ounce of humor left in him and because of this; she had long ago forgotten how to laugh.

"I...I just thought we should know because we *are* his foster parents."

"If you're so interested, then you ask him. Personally, I don't give a flying fuck."

He pushed her away from him.

"I told you not to get too close to me. I don't like to be crowded."

"I...I'm sorry John."

She paused.

"Is there *anything* you like about me anymore?" A guttural sob escaped her.

John Hoey looked at her for an instant and then turned and walked out of the apartment.

∽

The phone rang its muted ring. John Hoey had it set this way so it did not disturb "his space." His rules of engagement were for her to first make eye contact, before speaking.

"Hello?"

"My name is Hector Lopez. *Jour* son Danny has been spending time at my business, but I'm sure *jou* know this. He is a fine boy, which I'm sure *jou* also know. What I'm asking is that he stay overnight at my home, with my family. When I come over to *jour* house, *jou* can check me out and *jou* are also free to come to my business. It's on the same street as *jour* house, The Honor Boxing Club."

"I...I know where that is, and you can take him for whatever night you want. It's not necessary to come over here."

"Okay, fine, it'll be this Saturday and we'll bring him back Sunday after church." *Stuttering must run in this family*, thought Hector.

🌺 CHAPTER FIVE 🌺

On Saturday, Danny walked down to the club, unescorted as usual, from his white building. Hector and the two boys were waiting for him in the front of the Honor Club. "Closed for the Day" the sign on the door said.

"You have a n..nice car Hector."

"Thank you Danny."

The car, a nine year old Toyota Camry was kept clean, but had endured the vigor of daily trips from Queens into Manhattan. Its once dark blue color had, from lack of polish, faded to pale grey, and its doors were battle scarred from the war of the parking lots.

"My wife Marisol will have breakfast ready and you will get to meet my daughter Maria."

Danny looked out the window of the coveted front passenger seat. The struggle over that seat between Tito and Mario did not take place as they conceded the *shotgun* spot to Danny. His world was expanding with each turn and Hector was reluctant to break this spell with conversation..

The house was white with blue shutters and was a castle in Danny's eyes. Marisol and Maria were waiting at the front door. When the car pulled into the driveway they came out. By the time the Toyota stopped, they were standing at the front doors of the garage.

What a beautiful family I have, inside and out. Hector thought. *This is truly a great moment.*

Hector got out, kissed Marisol and hugged Maria before opening the passenger side door.

Danny threw off his seat belt and jumped out without looking, right into the waiting arms of Marisol. She had been told about the physical contact, but got caught up in the moment. Marisol was not the only one – Danny hugged her back. He bashfully shook Maria's hand, and she awkwardly shook it back.

"*Welcome to the Lopez house,*" Marisol said in Spanish, and was about to repeat it in English, when Danny answered back.

"*Gracias por invitarme a su casa.*"(Thank you for inviting me to your home)

The five Lopez members were caught by surprise, but only Hector noticed the omission of stuttering.

"I…I learned by myself. Th…the library at school had tapes and a teacher at school g…gave me her old tape machine. I…I used all the tapes at the library."

"Well you are a very smart boy," said Marisol. "I think your Spanish is very good." She had her hands on each of his shoulders. Danny looked sheepish, but did not pull away.

Breakfast consisted of eggs, any way. Danny had to be told the ways. There was sausage, bacon, pancakes and warm rolls. Tito got Hector off to the side. "This is one heck of a breakfast, could we adopt him?"

After breakfast, Maria took Danny out in the neighborhood to meet her friends. Later the boys had him for Frisbee and video games. Lunch was snacks, but dinner was more formal.

With each successive meal Danny's smile grew larger. He noted that this meal began a little different. All of the pre-meal banter had stopped. Danny was seated next to Marisol, who explained that they were thanking God for providing this meal and the wonderful life that they all have.

Everyone got quiet and Danny listened to the words that Marisol said. "And we thank God for bringing Danny here today to be part of our family."

I'm part of a family? He put his hands together, but was smart enough not to move them as they did.

"Don't worry about it Danny, I will show you how, and what it means," said Marisol, as she place her arm around him and spoke quietly into his ear.

∽

After the whole family took part in the dinner clean-up, Marisol took Danny off to the side. A catechism was taken from Maria's room. She explained the Trinity as it pertained to the sign of the cross."

"Are there three gods?"

"No," Marisol explained. *This is the toughest part, if he gets this, he's one smart child.* "There is only one God. Do you know what 'unity' means?"

"Yes I do. It means every body is together or something like that."

"That's great, Danny. You're absolutely right." *This kid is unbelievable.* "There is a Holy Spirit between God the Father and his son Jesus. And that's what we say when we make the sign of the cross; Father, Son, and the Holy Spirit."

Danny was completely absorbed by his new knowledge and Marisol promised to get him his own catechism.

I have never seen any one so thirsty to learn about religion. Not my children, not anybody's children. Marisol thought.

∞

Bedtime was heralded with "good nights" all around. Danny bunked in with the boys.

Lying next to each other, Hector turned toward Marisol. "I know what you want to say," she said. "Or I should say, I know what you want to ask."

"He's a good kid." Hector said.

"I know and the answer is, yes."

"And I knew that would be *jour* answer. It won't be easy; we're the wrong color, but I'm not going to let that stop us."

"It never has. When you got it going, you were unstoppable in the ring."

"How would *jou* know? *Jou* never saw *any* of my fights."

"I did once, before we were married. I went with a group of my friends to where you were fighting and we convinced the keeper of the gate to let us in to see you. We told him we would be right out. And we were. I saw you go after some guy after he had opened a cut over your right eye." She stroked his right eyebrow. "I cried and my friends took me out."

"*Jou're* so pretty. And I'm so lucky."

"I'm the lucky one. I got a brave man whose heroic *big heart* is the reason I love you so much."

❧ Chapter Six ❧

Weeks went by and then months. Danny had found his self-confidence, not only at the club, but at his school. All was well except that he longed for more time with his new family. The feeling was mutual.

Danny had adopted the Lopez family in spirit; Hector and Marisol had filed the application in earnest. Danny was given permission from Kerry Hoey for an extended stay with the Lopez family from Friday to Sunday night. "I..I th..think that will be fine. H..he seems happy with y..you." Kerry said into the phone receiver.

"Thank you Mrs. Hoey for your understanding and your love for Danny. Someday we will have to meet." Marisol responded.

Kerry Hoey did not respond.

They both said their goodbyes as the phone call was ended.

With her hand still on the receiver, Marisol turned to Hector, "said it would be all right. *Her* stuttering is getting worse as Danny's is disappearing."

Danny's routine was to go over to the club during the week and bring along his homework. When the weekend came all of him belonged to the Lopez's. After his homework was checked by Tito, Danny would follow Perkins all over the club. Hector was his father figure, but Perkins was his idol. When Perkins worked the heavy bag so did Danny, even though the bag took him for a ride. When Perkins shadow boxed, Danny was his shadow. Danny's skills on the speed bag were equal to any other club member, and along with Perkins, they sounded like a well synchronized drum team.

"Danny!" Perkins called from across the club. "Do you want to work the focus mitts with me?"

"Why wouldn't I?" His stuttering had all but left.

He pulled the mitts out of the bin and climbed into the ring. Danny stood for a moment, frozen in place. *The Ring*, that sacred area, where pugilists pounded out a reputation and gave hope to a downtrodden people. Here stood the gladiators of their day. Along with books on and about Catholicism and religion, he had devoured books on boxing and boxers. He could recite all of the glorious prose. Danny was struck by the moment, and the history that the ring represented.

"Let's go!" Perkins shouted – bringing Danny back to earth.

Perkins was fast, Danny was fast. It was a workout and a game at the same time.

At thirteen years old he was already beginning to fill out his young body. Danny had two parties for his October birthday; one at the club and another at the Lopez home. It was the first time that he could remember having a birthday celebration. "And I had two of them!" he exclaimed.

After the party at their house, Hector spoke with Marisol in their bedroom. "Next year I would like him to start high school where we live."

"Did they say how long the adoption procedure might take?" She asked.

"No, and they didn't seem happy to take my application. They asked me several times if *I* had filled it out, and told me that they could reject it if not properly done. I didn't tell them that *jou* did it. They said it could take a while for them to process it. They didn't say how long a while is. And this is just the *first* step in bringing Danny here. I got a funny feeling about this. I'm glad we decided not to tell him."

On Sunday night Danny was taken back to the Hoey's and on Monday, a rejection letter was delivered. Marisol called Hector who left the club and returned home.

"What does it say is the reason?" Hector asked.

"It was difficult to decipher, but it says in a veiled way that we're not a good fit. It doesn't directly say this, but this is what is meant."

Hector pounded his fist on the kitchen table. "We got knocked out in the first round." He stopped talking and began nodding his head.

"You have an idea?" Marisol asked.

"Maybe," he said, and stopped nodding his head.

Hector did not say what it was and she knew not to ask any further.

"I trust you Hector. I love you and I trust you."

He squeezed her tight.

"Mari, *jou* are my life."

❦ CHAPTER SEVEN ❧

"That *spic* is going to take the kid, and the money will go with him. I don't want to go through all that paperwork and the investigations again. We were lucky to get past that *once*. *And*, I don't want him to go there anymore, period! Do you understand me?"

"I..I don..don't think that's necessary, we're actually saving money."

"You don't think! And stop stuttering. It makes you look dumber then you already are."

"I hate you. I hate you," Kerry cried.

"You ugly bitch, you'll do as I say."

"I didn't always look this way. I was pretty when we first met. You made m..me look this way," she sobbed.

John Hoey faced her and poked his finger against her forehead. His body was solid from the years of working on the docks. He had also worked "on call" as an enforcer for a minor player in the mob.

"You don't ever give me your lip again." He pushed her backward with his finger, leaving an indent on her forehead.

As he left their apartment, Kerry called out in a mocking tone. "Say hello to Betty for me! Like I don't know!"

Hoey looked back into the apartment with a scowl. Kerry slammed the door shut without retaliation.

As dusk settled, Danny returned to the apartment. Kerry was waiting and offered him something to eat.

"We have apple pie or chocolate chip cookies. Which do you want, or you can have both?"

"No thanks, Kerry. I'm all 'desserted' up." He saw her look of disappointment. "But, I'll take a glass of milk, thanks. Did you bump your head or something?"

"Oh, it was the cabinet door. I opened it too fast. Maybe I should come with you and take some boxing lessons to learn how to duck."

She did not and could not tell him that he could no longer go to the club.

Danny had just finished his milk when John Hoey pushed open the apartment door – drunk.

"Well the prodigal son retuned. Did you tell him that he can't go there anymore?"

Kerry's silence answered his question.

"I didn't think so!"

"You can't go to that club anymore. Understand me? It's over." Hoey snarled.

"Y…you can't do that! I will…"

Danny was struck across his right eye with the back of Hoey's hand, before he could finish.

"You will do nothing. If you do, you'll go back to that sewer of a foster care holding tank. That's the only place you'll go. And you'll stay there too, because nobody's gonna want a teenager."

"B...better than here."

"Answering back? You little bastard!"

Hoey struck Danny, again, this time with a closed fist; across his right cheek and mouth.

Kerry came between them.

"Stop it! D..don't hit him again."

Hoey reeled back with his left fist and punched her right eye black. The apartment became quiet. Danny did not make any sound – his plan was escape. Kerry knew that any moan or whimper from her would attract another punch. It was an uneasy stillness that enveloped three people in the same dwelling. Danny in his room planning, Kerry lying in bed resigned to her fate, and Hoey next to her in an alcoholic induced sleep.

Hoey left before 8 a.m. When Danny came out to the kitchen for breakfast, Kerry was there waiting with both food and first aid. She could not show any concern for Danny, before, or it would have promoted further violence from Hoey.

"It's okay Kerry, I got up during the night and cleaned it up (the wounds) like I see Hector do for the boxers." His cheek was bruised and his lower lip was swollen. His right eye did not show any sign of Hoey's blow. "It was a glancing shot." Danny determined with an expert tone. Kerry was not so lucky. Her eye was swollen shut.

"Maybe you should come down to the Club and have Hector look at it? He was an army medic you know."

"Th..thanks Danny, but I don't want people to know that

John hits me. You're a good boy, who got a rotten deal. Don't tell John I told you, but *you* go down to the Club and see what can be done for you to stay there."

"What will happen to you?"

"D...don't worry about me. My life is how you see it. I...I'm no better than John Hoey. We're white trash and you deserve better."

"No, you're not. You're not like John at all."

❧ Chapter Eight ❧

Danny did not go to school, but stayed with Kerry until the end of the school day. They talked and shared their feelings, and their hurts. It was a conversation between two tortured inmates of John Hoey. While exposing their most sensitive thoughts, Danny and Kerry held hands across the kitchen table.

"I didn't know what was going on when they told me my parents weren't coming home. I didn't know what they meant. When the next day came and I didn't see them, I knew."

Kerry failed to hold back her tears as she listened. She told of *her* coming from a broken home; no high school diploma and John Hoey, maybe, being a way out.

"Guess not." She half smiled.

At 3 p.m., it was time for the school to "let out" and time for Danny to leave for the Club.

"Danny?" Kerry called out.

"John Hoey is a dangerous man."

As young as Danny was, he knew why she said this.

Looking back into the apartment, Danny waved and said, "thank you."

❧ Chapter Nine ❧

Danny walked through the door and Hector's look of joy changed immediately to a face of anguish; his heart dropping to the breaking point.

"Who did this to *jou* my son?"

Danny went to Hector and cried in his arms. Hector held onto him; his anger momentarily put on hold.

Bobby Perkins came running over.

"It's that Hoey guy, am I right? I know what he looks like."

"Good. *Jou* go over and hang around that apartment, and when he gets home *jou* come and get me. *Jou* don't touch him; *jou* can't touch him. *Jou* know that!"

"You can't either Pops."

"*Jou* don't worry about me, there are other ways to take care of this."

"Good, I was worried, but you know the law better than me."

Perkins left to perform his guard duty.

"I…I didn't mean for this to happen. I…I'm sorry, I'm sorry." Danny cried.

"What have *jou* got to be sorry about? Being born? *Jou* know we are trying to adopt *jou*. *Jou* will be my son – no different from Tito or Mario. *Jou* even speak Spanish, how good is that?" Hector smiled.

Danny's weak smile was forced.

At this point, the front door was flung open and Perkins was standing in the entranceway.

"He's home."

"*Jou* take care of Danny, I got some things to straighten out with Mr. Hoey."

"Be careful, Pops. Please remember the law; I need you."

"I told *jou* not to worry I'm just going to talk and threaten him with the cops." *Talk my ass, I'm going to take this fucking guy apart.*

Perkins let Hector get in full stride before following him at a distance.

Hector was at their door. He knocked, but wasn't going to give anymore time for a second knock.

Kerry opened the door, revealing her swollen black eye; then stood to the side.

Hector pushed it wider and stepped into the foyer which opened into the living room. Hoey was standing in the middle and at 6'3" took up most of the small area.

"So is this a neighborly call, Pancho? Or are you at the wrong address for your illegal alien meeting?" Hoey spoke with a menacing tone.

Hector moved toward him and ducked as a small chair was hurled; clipping him in the forehead. Hoey followed the chair with a wild punch to Hector's head. Hector moved his head back and the blow landed on his shoulder.

"You think you're dealing with some amateur? You *spics* are all alike, no brains."

Hector assumed a fighter's stance, fists in front and moved in. Hoey's eyes widened.

Two quick lefts to Hoey's right side broke a rib, the follow up right cross broke Hoey's jaw and the left hook after that, broke his nose.

Sitting on the floor in front of his sofa spitting blood, Hoey cried out. "You're in deep shit. You can't…" he spit more blood. "You can't use your fists like…" he spit, more blood.

"*Jou* listen to me *jou* piece of shit. *Jou* are going to take *jourself* to the hospital and tell them *jou* were in a car accident. If *jou* don't have a car, buy one. If *jou* don't have any money, steal one. If *jou* say anything about me, I will come back here, or wherever *jou* are, and *jou* will wish *jou* were dead."

"I will say you defended me, Mr. Lopez." Kerry spoke out.

"I'll take her to where ever you think it's safe Pops." Perkins was standing in the doorway.

Hector's head snapped toward the voice of Perkins. He then put his foot on Hoey's chest. "Don't make me have to come back."

Kerry packed her belongings and left the apartment with Hector and Perkins.

"I know a good friend that *jou* could stay with for a while. *Jou* will be safe there."

He made a telephone call and then gave her the address. "She says *jou* can stay as long as *jou* want."

Back at the club, Perkins' training session began again. No one else was told of what took place at the Hoey apartment, which made Perkins feel even closer to Hector.

Perkins covered over his mouth with his boxing mitt and said, in a low voice.

"You told me you were going to be careful – now what?"

"It was a one time elimination fight. I eliminated the other fighter and now I'm back retired. Sorry about not following *jour* non- violent plan, but don't worry, Mr. Hoey is not in a position to be calling in the cops."

"From what I saw, you're a one man wrecking machine and the boxing world should be very happy that you remain retired; their titles are safe."

"*Jou* see too much. It wasn't a fair contest. He didn't have a good trainer like *jou* do."

✖ CHAPTER TEN ✖

The office was on the eighth floor on 28th street; they had offices all over the city. Hector chose not to use the elevator.

"Social Services" was boldly etched on the door. The whole building was Social Services, but this was the section that handled special cases.

Hector had told Marisol earlier, "Mari, how come the only time we're a special case is when we're *not* going to get any special treatment." They both laughed.

Hector announced to the gum chewing receptionist that he had an appointment with Mrs. White. The receptionist, who had chalky white skin and severely short blonde hair, did not speak, but continued to chew gum; ever so often snapping a bubble within her mouth. When she got up from behind her desk, Hector could only hope that she was going for Mrs. White.

Mrs. White did not smile when she extended her hand to Hector. Nor did she exchange any pleasantries other than, "I'm Mrs. White." She got right to business.

"There are many white families looking for foster care

children and for adoption. We can't fill all of the requests we have for white children. Would you consider a black child?"

The desk sign said Mrs. White; Mrs. White was black. *I wonder if her first name is Lillian; that would really be something.* Hector *thought* he had only smiled to himself.

"Do you find some amusement in what I'm saying Mr. Lopez?"

"First of all *jou* aren't listening. We KNOW this kid. He stays at our house. And for the record, I'm Hispanic not black. At least that's what *jou* would have me check off on *jour* form."

"I'm sorry Mr. Lopez, I have my guidelines and I have to follow them. I'm not saying there is a law preventing this adoption; I'm just saying that all other avenues would have to be exhausted before we would grant it. You say that he is thirteen? Well it would be years before all this is settled. By then it wouldn't matter."

"Man *jou* got some job Mrs. White. All is black and white to *jou*. What about feelings, what about heart, what about love?"

"I'm afraid those are not in the guidelines and they never will be. You're just going to have to get a grip on yourself and be resigned to reality."

I'll tell jou who I'd like to get a grip on. Hector said to himself.

"Thank *jou* Mrs. White. I can't say that *jou* have been helpful, but *jou* just make me want to fight harder."

Hector turned away from her and went to the door. He turned back, "*Jou* have the wrong sign on the door!"

"How is *that* Mr. Lopez?"

"It should say, 'Social Services Special Cases – People of Color Need Not Apply.' And on the second line, 'See Mrs. White.' How cool is that?"

He turned and walked away. His huge grin was the last image she would see.

Hector's grin quickly disappeared as he went out of view.

They are stopping this poor kid from having a good life, he said to no one. *Marisol...maybe Marl will have an idea.* He returned to the Club for the rest of the day.

∽

The house was quiet. Hector and Marisol's bedroom was on the first floor; all of the other bedrooms were on the second floor. "Tito and Maria seem good with this, I don't know about Mario, but I'm sure he'll come around." Marisol said to the ceiling and to Hector lying beside her.

"We won't be able to keep him," said Hector, ignoring Marisol's comment.

"You're making your blood pressure go up. They just can't keep giving you the next highest dosage." Marisol said.

"I can't help it. I think I was born with high blood pressure. I worry about everything, but never as much as adopting Danny. The headaches are starting again. No dreams, but I wake up with flashes going off. I know they're muzzle flashes, but there isn't any noise."

"Please, you are scaring me, Hector. I thought that was left behind years ago."

"It was, but it wasn't buried too deep. And now with this, its come back."

"I will check at my school in the morning and see if anyone has heard of this type of adoption." Marisol said.

"Okay, that sounds good. I don't get many boxing lawyers, but I'll ask around and find out if anybody has a cousin that is one."

It wasn't long before Hector drifted off to sleep *No matter what, he never did have any trouble getting to sleep.* Marisol thought and smiled. It faded quickly as she stayed awake listening to his heart beat. *Such a good heart, please Lord, please give us this boy to love.* Lying on her back, tears came from the corner of each eye and rolled down her cheeks.

❧ CHAPTER ELEVEN ❧

In the morning Hector opened the Club as usual, but he was unable to concentrate; leaving Perkins in charge, he felt that he needed some fresh air – something not generated at a boxing gym. He went for what he often referred to as, his therapeutic walk. The solitude and the change of scenery usually helped clear a path to the problem, and when he was finished, he would have walked his way to a solution. This time it was different. He did not have a flight plan for this walk; he was just walking. His mantra was, "I can't let this happen." This time, he was trying to walk *away* from the problem.

From The Honor Club on Fifteenth Street, he turned south on the Avenue of the Americas (Sixth Avenue). He continued on this straight path as he crossed over Canal Street and Sixth Avenue became Church Street. When Hector crossed over to Church Street, his gait took on a deliberate stride. What started out as a aimless journey, became a forced march to the Woolworth Building at 233 Broadway. He walked left on Park Place and right on Broadway, placing him at the front doors of the Woolworth Building; a total trip of almost three miles.

Hector stood on the marble floor and looked up at the directory. He found the "Office of New York State Senator Charles Marchand" – in bold letters. His office was on the fourth floor. This time Hector took the elevator.

The doors closed, and at mach speed, opened to the fourth floor; two doors down on the right, suite 404, the glass door read the same as the directory, "Offices of New York State Senator Charles Marchand." It was etched in gold. The last time he saw Charlie "Duke" Marchand he had etching from shrapnel drawn across his chest. After that, the lieutenant's war was over; unlike Homer's "only the dead have seen the end of war." Lieutenant Charles Marchand was lucky to go back to a life to which he was born – privileged.

They wouldn't let him in. Mrs. Conroy was adamant about this. There were two desks in front of the senator's door and Hector knew that he chose the wrong one.

"You can't just come into the Senator's office and expect to be seen. You must have an appointment – if *you* could get one."

If jou could get one, Hector repeated to himself, and then spoke. "*Jou* mean someone like *me*, don't *jou* Mrs. Conroy?"

He did not wait for a reply, but instead went to the other desk. The second desk sign read "Ms. Ramirez." He took a chance.

"*Oiste lo que paso con ese?*" (You heard what went on with *that* one.) Hector moved his eyes toward Mrs. Conroy. "*Nesecito hablar con el Senator – es muy imporatante* "(I need to see the Senator badly – it is very important) *"Si, es possible, dile que Doc estat afuero para ver Duke."* (If you could, please tell him that *Doc* is outside to see *Duke*.)

Ms. Ramirez did not immediately get up from her desk, so as not to give Hector away. *There's something about this guy that speaks the truth; that, and I can't stand the bitch I work with,* she thought. She called in to Marchand's office, saying that she was bringing in the papers he wanted. The intercom spoke back, asking her to please come in.

Hector knew the man behind the voice.

After handing him the documents, she remained standing at the front of Marchand's desk.

"Is there something else Carmen?"

"Yes I…I have someone outside who says to tell you that 'Doc' is here to see 'Duke.'"

Senator Charles Marchand dropped his pen. His facial expression changed from its usual public on-camera look to borderline emotional.

"He's actually right outside?"

"Yes he is."

"My God! Please send him in."

Hector followed Carmen into the office. Marchand smiled at her and nodded his signal to close the door behind as she left. As the door closed Marchand was out from behind his desk. Tears flowed from both grown men as they embraced for the worst of times and the best of everlasting bonding.

Marchand spoke first. "I've thought about you a lot; especially with this war in Iraq being up front in the news. You saved my life, Hector."

"We were just kids thrown together from different lives

and then we went back to those lives." Hector paused, "The ones that could go back."

Without fanfare they both stopped to reflect to that time and to the names that did not return.

"I followed *jour* career in the papers and I was proud that I knew *jou* for maybe the toughest time of *jour* life."

"You're not saying that I lead a charmed life, are you?" Marchand was smiling.

"No, I was happy that the 'Duke' was having a *royal* life." They both smiled at that one.

"I see that your command of English has gotten much better."

"It had to, I married a teacher."

"I too saw your name in the paper after you made it back…" Marchand paused and swallowed hard. "I guess you fought for a while and then I didn't see your name anymore, or at least it wasn't you that was in the papers. There are more than a few fighters by the name of Hector Lopez. I figured you would be too old to be one of them."

"Too old, *Jou* got that right! When we got back from Nam, we were all twenty years older than everyone else our age. I quit when I got married. Marisol didn't like it and wanted a family. One reason would have been good enough to quit."

"*Marisol*, that's a pretty name."

"Inside and out," said Hector.

There was a pause.

"I have a problem, Duke. There's a little boy that I want to adopt, but it seems they're short on the color white these days and want to use up their black inventory first. His name is Danny McCoy – he's white and we love him like our own."

≈

Marchand went for his intercom. "Mrs. Conroy, could you please come into the office?"

Diane Conroy was through the office door in an instant.

"Mrs. Conroy, did Mr. Lopez try to come into my office from your desk?"

"Yes, but…" Marchand interrupted.

"Your intercom button is stuck again. I couldn't hear Mr. Lopez, but I could certainly hear you. Please un-stick it when you go back out, but before you do, take a good look at Mr. Lopez. He is to be afforded all privileges possible as a holder of our nation's highest honor – The Congressional Medal of Honor. He is to be granted access to my office at any time. I don't care if the President is in here, I don't care if Jesus Christ himself is in here. He gets in! Do you understand?"

"Yes," Conroy said in a weak voice.

"It is not the fact that you didn't know who he was, it is the fact that you decided who he *is*, that caused you to predetermine your actions."

Conroy nodded without a sound.

"I have a project for you. Our job, as you know, is to help the citizens of New York with their problems, especially problems with government agencies. And Mr. Lopez, here, is having trouble with one of them. You are to contact Social Services and work with a Mrs. White. I will give you the full names, addresses and telephone numbers of all the agencies that you will be dealing with. *We* are going to fast track an adoption so that Danny McCoy will become Mr. Lopez's son."

Conroy blinked.

"When Mr. Lopez leaves, I will fill you in on all of the particulars. You will be working along *with* Ms. Ramirez. That will be all for now. Oh, and don't forget to call a repairman for the intercom."

The door closed behind Mrs. Conroy, and "Duke" Marchand turned his attention to Hector, who was seated on the chair along side his desk. His face was buried in his hands.

"It'll be fine, Hector. Your ordeal is over. So is Mrs. Conroy, who unfortunately, I will have to promote to get rid of her."

❧ CHAPTER TWELVE ❧

Four months later, the adoption took place. During that time, and with Senator Marchand's intervention, Danny was allowed to stay with the Lopez family until the adoption was finalized. He started high school at the same time as Maria; Tito and Mario were upper classmen at Commerce High School in Queens.

Although Danny was told that it was not necessary, he asked that his name be changed to Danny Lopez. "I know who my mother and father were, and will always love them, but now I'm part of a new family, and I don't want to be different."

Hector and Marisol noted that everyone appeared to be happy with Danny's decision except Mario. They were reluctant to speak to him about it, and decided that the less said would be best.

∾

Getting adapted to new school surroundings was not something new for Danny, and for once, his experience in foster care was helpful. He was beginning a new school without stuttering, however, the start was not without incident.

On the first day of classes, Luis Perez, who had known Maria from their middle school, came through a crowd of high energy freshmen, to confront her and Danny in the hallway. "What you do'in with that white kid Maria? You giv'n him some of your pussy?"

Danny leapt at him and struck him on the chin with a straight right. Although outweighing Danny by over fifty pounds, he was knocked backwards into the wall lockers. Luis sprung off of the lockers and into the path of Tito. Luis' eyes widened with fear as he looked to see what Maria might say.

"He insulted me, Tito, and said some terrible things."

Although they were of the same weight and height, the comparisons ended there.

Going face to face with Luis, Tito spoke, "If this ever happens again, I promise, I will make you cry in front of all your friends. Tito eyed the crowd, but to no one in particular. "Don't ever fuck with my sister or my brother Danny again."

"Okay, I'm cool bro, I'm cool."

"No Luis, you're not cool, and you're not my brother; he is." He pointed to Danny. Luis turned and left, without making any more eye contact.

"You should have seen Danny knock Luis into the lockers." Her eyes shined like her mother's.

"You did good Danny," said Tito. Turning to Maria, he added, "And don't tell Dad what I just said to Luis."

Maria nodded and said, "How can I, I'm not allowed to say that word."

Tito smiled, gave her thumbs up and winked at her.

∾

When Danny turned sixteen, he asked if he could enter the New York Daily News Golden Gloves. Danny's birthday celebration took place around the dinner table; *his* choice – to spend it at home with his family. Maria's sixteenth birthday was next month and Hector and Marisol had rented out a catering hall. As usual all dinner discussions were in the open and all decisions were open for discussion.

"His education must come first. He may be a talented boxer, which is not for me to judge, but he *is* a talented scholar. This I *can* attest to." Marisol proclaimed, and added. "He's an honor student, and I wouldn't want him to slide from that. I have high hopes that he will achieve anything that he sets his mind to. I don't want that beautiful brain rattled. You once quit for me Hector, please think this out too."

"Mom, I promise you, if you let me box, I will keep my grades up. I have goals too, and they are to win the Golden Gloves and get a college degree. I don't want to be a professional boxer, but I *do* want to prove to myself, that I could have if I wanted to."

It was a strong argument and both Tito and Maria looked as if they wanted to applaud.

Hector was equally pleased with Danny's response, while Mario's face remained unchanged and expressionless.

"Okay then, we'll start *jour* amateur career, so that *jou* can eventually enter the 'open class;' winning in that class will be *jour* proof."

ॐ

    In the next few months Danny's workout at the Club was no different than that of the other fighters, except that he had a team working with him. Bobby Perkins was assigned to him on a full time basis. After twenty-five wins and five losses (none of the losses were while he was with The Honor Boxing Club), Bobby Perkins was dealt a blow that he could not duck. A routine exam revealed a spot on his lung. An operation was ordered, and along with the cancerous growth, part of his lung was removed; his boxing days were over. Hector knew that he could not depend upon his sons forever, so he offered Perkins a job as his assistant.

❧ CHAPTER THIRTEEN ❧

For his first amateur fight, in the 165 pound middle weight class, it looked to Danny as if his high school in Queens had taken over this Long Island arena. He felt awkward as he limbered up by shadow boxing and dancing around the ring; wondering how it looked to the crowd. *Do I look like a real fighter or a pretend one,* he thought. The introductions were made, and again, Danny felt embarrassed by receiving thunderous applause. They touched gloves and the crowd disappeared.

The kid with the Russian name came straight at him. Danny could see that Igor, Ivan or something that sounded like that lacked your basic skills. The Russian missed wildly, but Danny did not. He drove two lefts into his stomach and a solid right to his chin. As the kid with the Russian name fell backward from this barrage, he tried a desperate right hand – a bad choice. Danny went up over his right and caught him flush on his right cheek. A blow that head gear was not made to protect. The Russian met the canvass with a bounce, and the referee immediately, waved the fight over. Danny had won by a TKO in the first round.

"*Jou* did good son. *Jour* not always going to be taller, in fact, *jou* will probably be shorter when *jou* grow into the light heavyweight class," said Hector.

Bobby Perkins drove them all back to the house, Hector, Tito and Danny. Tito had alerted Marisol by cell phone (she would not prematurely assume victory) Mario did not attend the fight, saying that he would help his mother with the victory celebration. Hector knew that his mentioning of a *victory* celebration was his way of easing out of not wanting to go. Hector left it alone.

∞

The after fight parties lessened after each amateur bout, but resumed its fanfare with Danny's first Golden Gloves match. He was now eighteen years old, out of high school and had six amateur fights; winning them all by knockout. He went through his opponents in the "Gloves" as he did with his other bouts, eventually facing a fighter by the name of Oscar Juarez, in the semi-final of the 165-lb. Novice Class. Although they weighed the same, Juarez had a more compact build, because Danny had not yet gained the weight for his height.

Juarez pushed him all over the ring to an eventual win by decision.

"We'll fight him again someday. Don't *jou* worry, Danny. *Jou* got nothing to be ashamed of. The judges must have been counting pushes as punches, because if it were punches they were counting, *jou* would have won."

They had a "Golden Gloves Party," anyway.

Juarez lost by TKO in the finals, to a brash, trash talking fighter from Brooklyn, named Travis Smalls.

∾

Next year, Danny went into the Golden Gloves with six more amateur fights under his belt, all won by knockout. He had also competed in the Empire State Games, but to the dismay of his teammates, could not join them in the final round because he had gotten the flu.

He was fighting in the 178-lb Novice Class. This would be his last time fighting as a Novice. For all future years he will have qualified to fight in the Open Class. On his way to these finals Danny had 3 knockouts, 1 decision and 1 bye. His opponent in the finals was Oscar Juarez, who had also moved up in weight.

"He moved up in weight class, but it looks like all fat to me." Hector noted.

The finals were held at Madison Square Garden. After fighting all of the preliminary bouts in high schools, boxing clubs and sports centers, the magnitude of "The Garden" was overwhelming. Danny climbed into the ring and forced himself to look out at the crowd.

There are so many faces, so many that they seemed smeared, Danny thought. He looked away, glad, in a way, that he could not make out anyone familiar.

The announcements were made and the bell rang. Danny tried to get in close to work on Juarez' body, but was pushed back. Danny stayed on the outside and now it was Juarez who closed in, only to push away, again. Aside from a couple of outside jabs from Danny, the round was more of the same pushing tactics from Juarez.

At the end of the round, Danny looked up at Hector.

"The next time he pushes, *jou* come under his arm and

hit him with an uppercut to his right triceps." Although a natural right hander for eating, writing and boxing, Danny threw a ball with his left arm, and it was his strongest.

The bell rang for the second round and Danny took the first opportunity to follow Hector's instructions. Juarez extended his arms to push Danny away and Danny took one step to the left, and drove a left uppercut into Juarez's right triceps. When Juarez's arm dropped, Danny came over the top with a straight left and then plowed his right glove into Juarez's soft middle, making him stumble backwards. The ropes stopped Juarez's unbalanced retreat, and Danny took this advantage to pounce on a fighter in disarray. Lefts and rights were unanswered causing the referee to step in and stop the fight. Danny was the 178-lb Novice Champion.

❧ CHAPTER FOURTEEN ❧

At the completion of each of Danny's fights, the Lopez family would immediately begin its focus on the next bout. All family members were ready participants except Mario, who now had a girlfriend, and spent time away from the home. Even Marisol was excited about this upcoming "open" fight, selfishly, because she knew it would be Danny's last, but mostly, because winning it would fulfill Danny's dream.

Danny's presence at The Honor Boxing Club had attained celebrity status. He was their only champion, albeit being as an amateur. When he sparred in the ring, most of the other members lessened their intensity and they would go through their routines with one eye on Danny. Bobby Perkins and Hector were with him constantly, and the three of them would critique each sparring session.

"*Jou* are going to do fine Danny. There's nothing else that I can show *jou*," Hector spoke, while his hands were placed on Danny's shoulders. "*Jou* will see, my son, *jou* will see."

❧

The Lopez house, although consumed with Danny's

quest, was still organized around its maturing children. Maria was attending Molloy College out on Long Island, where she was in its nursing program. She was originally going to attend The School of Nursing of St. Vincent's on Staten Island, until her closest friend Amy and her family moved to Long Island. Together since grammar school, Maria worked out a way to be with her through college.

"Maybe someday we could even work at the same hospital?"

Maria would take the subway to Penn Station and then take the Long Island Railroad to the Rockville Centre station, where Amy would be waiting with her car. Hector was happy to have one of his children interested in the medical field.

Tito and Mario were taking classes at John Jay College, Tito for Criminal Justice, with the goal of becoming a New York City Police Officer, and Mario for Fire Science, and looking to take the next New York City Fireman test.

Danny had decided that he wanted to be a teacher, but because of his training for the Golden Gloves, he was not on a full time schedule. His college of choice was St. John's University.

Marisol had gone back to teaching and because of Danny's successes, the Honor Boxing Club was brimming with young boxers.

❧ CHAPTER FIFTEEN ❧

The active Lopez family made Danny's year pass quickly. He, again, entered the New York Daily News Golden Gloves. At almost twenty years old, Danny had filled out his 6'1" frame and had met the experience qualifications to compete in the "open class." His second trip to Madison Square Garden had not lost its thrill. Danny's opponent, last year's champion, Travis Smalls, had won all his bouts by knockout, as did Danny. The newspapers were hailing this bout as the future of boxing; more than just an amateur boxing match. Not aware of Danny's plans concerning his boxing career, the newspapers were heralding a rivalry not unlike Sugar Ray Robinson and Jake La Motta; one which would follow them into the professional boxing arena.

ॐ

"Ladies and Gentlemen," the announcer bellowed through the microphone, "The New York Daily News Golden Gloves Finals in the 178-lb Open Division. Fighting out of the gold corner, 'Mr. Excitement' himself, and last years 178-lb Open Champion, Travis 'Lights Out' Smalls. Travis has knocked out all of his opponents in this tournament, hails from The Bronx, and is representing the Seymour Avenue Gym. And fighting out of the blue corner for the first time in the Open Class, last years 178-lb Novice Champion, who on his way here, has also won each bout by knockout, Danny 'The Real McCoy' Lopez. He is representing The Honor Boxing Club."

The crowd was equally divided and cheered wildly after each boxer was announced. It then settled into a low buzz of anticipation.

The announcer began again.

"At this time I would like everyone to observe a moment of silence as the bell tolls ten times in honor of our brave servicemen and women who have lost their lives in the defense of our great country." The crowd grew still and the bell tolled ten times.

"Thank you. Thank you. And now I would like to indulge you one more time to honor one of our own heroes, Hector Lopez."

Hector snapped his head around to look at his sons, who were now looking in three different directions.

"You know him," the announcer continued, "as the owner of The Honor Boxing Club and former middleweight contender. But what you may not know, is that when he was sent to Vietnam from his native land of Puerto Rico, Hector came back a hero. Ladies and gentlemen," he paused and emphasized, "Hector Lopez earned our country's highest honor. He was awarded the Congressional Medal of Honor."

The crowd rose to its feet followed by a thunderous ovation.

Hector, sheepishly, stepped to the middle of the apron and extended his right arm to acknowledge the applause. When he moved back to Danny's corner, Marisol was there to greet him.

"*Jou* knew all about this?"

"It was all part of the conspiracy." She pointed him to the front row, where Maria stood applauding and crying. He grabbed her by her shoulders and brought her in close. The wetness from her cheeks removed all feelings of being "set up" by his sons.

"I have the best family," Hector managed to say through his emotion.

"I'm going to leave now," Marisol whispered.

"I understand, Mari. I'll see *jou* at home."

The fighters moved around the ring to loosen up. As they passed each other a second time, Travis said through clenched teeth, "You never fight nobody like me; your white ass is mine. What are you anyway, a *mick* or a *spic*?"

Danny just smiled and shadow boxed on by.

The referee called Travis and Danny to the center of the ring to hear the final instructions. The traditional stare down was Travis' sneer to Danny's semi-smile. Danny's raised eyebrows under his head gear could not be seen. The signal sounded for all to vacate the ring except for the boxers.

The bell rang and the fighters moved to the center – this time not to perform a forced ritual. At 6'4" Travis fulfilled Hector's prophesy of Danny being in the ring with taller fighters.

Danny missed two left hooks as Travis came up over the top with a straight right to Danny's jaw. Travis' look was one of triumph. Speaking through his mouthpiece, Travis told Danny, "You're nuth'n."

Danny blocked two more straight rights and then he closed the distance. Before Travis could move Danny fired three strong lefts to Travis' rib cage. Danny looked into Travis' eyes and saw him wince. This seemed to set off an animal like rage in Travis as he threw lefts and rights at Danny, backing him into the ropes as the round ended.

Danny sat on his stool placed by Bobby Perkins as Hector climbed through the ropes to be in front of Danny.

"*Jou* got his attention and *jou did* hurt him. Now *jou* have to watch his…his…" Hector grabbed at his chest and went to one knee. *I can't waste any time,* he quickly thought.

"Tito! *Jou* have to get me to a hospital."

With Tito on one side and Bobby on the other they took Hector out of the ring.

"Dad!" Danny cried out; tears welling in his eyes.

Hector called out to Mario.

"It's *jour* time now, son. It's *jour* time."

Mario looked at his father being supported by Tito and Bobby, and then back to Danny. He saw the anguish over their father in Danny's eyes. *Our father,* he said to himself.

Mario climbed through the ropes just as the signal was given for seconds to get out. Danny went out for round two without any directions; this had never happened to him before.

Travis had witnessed this from his corner across the ring. They met in the center as before.

"Who's your daddy now?" Travis taunted. He then let loose a torrent of punches. Danny was not prepared for this onslaught and too preoccupied to put up a decent defense.

He fell against the ropes as Travis rained punch after punch at a seemingly defenseless Danny.

The referee stepped in and afforded Danny a standing eight count. A puffed up Travis Small, went to the neutral corner.

At the end of the count, Travis went back to working over Danny. Many of his punches were blocked and Danny's response was a feeble attempt at throwing no more then a weak jab. Just before the end of the second round, a straight right to the jaw put Danny on rubbery legs. He didn't think his knees would support him, so he pitched forward onto the apron with both knees and gloves to keep him from rolling over. Travis was jumping up and down all the way to the neutral corner as the referee began his count. At the count of seven Danny's head and body had recovered sufficiently to push himself to his feet. The referee asked Danny if he could go on, he looked into his eyes and wiped off his gloves. He then waved the fight to continue just as the bell sounded ending the round.

Mario put the stool down for Danny and then stood with his hands on his shoulders.

"I'm so sorry for the sorry ass way I treated you. It took *this* to see how much of a son you are to Dad and how much of a brother you are to me. Please forgive me. I can't tell you any more then Dad has already told you, but this I can tell you. Travis thinks that because he's black he's automatically tougher. Not so, Danny. You probably had a much tougher beginning then he did and you had something else that he didn't have. You had me to make you miserable."

"I never noticed. All I know is that you were not like Tito, but you were still my brother."

"You're a better man than me Danny. And I know you're a better fighter then Travis. Go out there and let him know what a Lopez is made of."

The bell rang for the third round and Travis was set to begin where he had left off. His confidence level was elevated along with his cockiness. Based on the last round he figured Danny was through. Danny put in a feeble jab with his right hand as Travis, thinking more of the same from the last round, came boring in. Travis was swinging with roundhouse lefts and rights, clipping Danny on his arms. When the second roundhouse right went by, Danny ducked under it and put every ounce of strength behind his left as he powered it into Travis' rib cage. Danny could tell that this blow had done some serious damage. Travis' right arm went instinctively down to protect his ribs, and his head came up, and for a split second their faces came together. Danny saw fear in Travis' eyes just before they were closed by Danny's right uppercut. Travis fell backwards; his head bouncing off of the canvas. The referee stood over Travis who was sprawled, spread eagle, in the middle of the ring. He took out Travis' mouthpiece and waved the fight over, as a triumphant Danny was lifted up by his brother.

"I guess I'm the 'Real McCoy' now?" Danny said.

"No you're not; you're the 'Real Lopez.'" Mario countered.

The celebration was short lived. Danny put on his sweats without showering and hovered over Mario who was on his cell phone.

"He's at St. Vincent's Hospital." Mario reported.

The tournament officials understood what had happened

and knew that Danny wasn't staying around for the victory gathering. They also took the initiative to have a taxi waiting for Danny and Mario.

Standing outside the main entrance of St. Vincent's was Bobby Perkins.

Before Danny and Mario were completely out of the taxi, Perkins spoke, "He's doing fine. Your mother, Tito and Maria are with him now."

"Thank God!" Danny and Mario almost said in unison.

Hector was sitting up in the hospital bed with Marisol and Maria on each side. Tito had been called down to the lobby.

"It was a reaction to his new blood pressure medicine." Marisol said.

"Hey Champ!" Hector opened up his arms for Danny to enter. Danny held him tight and wept on his shoulder.

"I'm sorry, I'm sorry. I can't help it." Danny said through quivering lips.

Jou can't help it Danny, we are all very emotional in the Lopez family. So it's in *jour* genes."

Hector then turned his attention to Mario. As their heads came together, Hector spoke into Mario's ear. "*Jou* did good son, I knew that *jou* would"

"Thanks for being patient, Dad, I love you." Mario whispered back.

There was then a commotion at the door to Hector's private room. Tito along with two tournament officials, in tow, entered the room with Danny's trophy. Following up the rear, was a cameraman. Tito had been asked by those officials to keep them informed of Hector's condition. When it was determined that he did not have a heart attack, as all signs had earlier indicated, they asked if they could come to the hospital.

The diamond-studded Gold Gloves was given to Hector and in turn it was given to Danny; all done with the video rolling.

The rivalry that was heralded by the newspapers was not to be. It had been settled during the tournament. As Hector was referred to as Pops, Danny from this time on, became "champ."

❧ Chapter Sixteen ❧

In the ensuing twelve years, the Lopez family aged into solid vocations and extended families. Danny became the God Father of Mario and Colleen's boy Hector Lopez II, while Mario was the God Father of Tito and Trisha's boy, Daniel. Tito was a New York City Policeman and Mario a New York City Firefighter.

Maria married a New York City Policeman, whom she met through Tito, and two years later gave birth to Hector and Marisol's first granddaughter. She continued to work part-time as an R.N. for Special Needs patients.

Danny was a high school teacher and taught history at Hicksville High School on Long Island. His rented house in Oyster Bay, Long Island, put him in driving distance to his job. But on most Sundays, they all converged for dinner at their original home in Queens.

∾

The house was crowded as it usually was on most Sundays.

"Hey Bro, when are you going to bring around one of your *models*?" Mario kidded Danny.

"Now how can I bring anyone here that would meet the standards you guys set with your wives? I'm talking about brains *and* class."

"You *see* Mario, 'brains and class,' he didn't mention anything about bodies. Your brother Danny has style." Colleen said in a mock scolding way.

"Yeah well that's all well and good. Ask him why all of these so called brainy and classy girls are all size one." Mario said, emphasizing it by pointing his index finger in the air.

At that point they all joined in to poke fun at Danny.

"Dinner!" Marisol called from the kitchen.

After eating, the girls remained in the dining room and kitchen; cleaning up and getting ready for dessert. The men headed to the den.

"Now that school is out, I'm looking for a job that could carry me through the summer months. Anyone hear about anything like that; that I could do?" As soon as Danny said it, he knew that he left himself open to zingers. And it was instantaneous.

"Until you mentioned 'something that I can do,' I thought I could help. But that kind of knocked you right out of any job I could think of," answered Mario.

At that remark, Danny got up from his seat on the sofa and made like he was going to hit Mario. Tito spoke up, "If you hit him, I'm going to have to arrest you, but only after you hit him at least twice."

Hector sat back and reveled in the banter from his sons. It never failed to entertain him and for him, it was better than the dessert, which was on the way.

When the wisecracking died down, Tito spoke up. "Okay, okay, I'm being serious here. I know a cop who I work with that has this job at a restaurant/club, formerly an all men's club. He's looking for someone to take this job for the summer, so that his wife could work. It would be perfect for you Danny."

"That good, that's good, but if it's for security, I may not qualify," said Danny.

"'May not,' are the magic words here Danny. As far as I know, you don't need security training or any kind of a license. All he does, according to him, is to make sure the bouncers are doing their job and that the waitresses are not harassed by the patrons." Tito answered.

"You said, 'former all men's club,' what did you mean by that?" Danny asked.

Tito looked as if he wished he didn't have to answer this question. "To be direct with you Danny, the place was once a strip club." Tito was quick to add. "My buddy says it *was* a strip club and now there isn't any signs of its past. It's now a sports bar and an Italian restaurant."

"Oh that's great!" Danny exclaimed.

Hector sat there and rolled his eyes. The boys talked about things in front of him, because they knew he would not interject his opinion. They had *his* respect and by allowing him to listen in on their life, he knew that he had *their* respect.

"They pay two hundred a night," said Tito and paused. "Not a bad chunk of change."

"Okay, you can tell him about me. I'll take a look – if it's as you say, I'll take it, as long as I don't have to wear a thong." He playfully slapped Mario on the cheek before he could say anything. He turned to Tito. "Arrest me!"

When the laughing subsided, dessert was ready.

❧ CHAPTER SEVENTEEN ❧

The building was located on Eighth Avenue in mid-town New York; in an area that was undergoing a period of morphing, from the bare skin of strip clubs, to the overdressed style of New York City fashions. Clothing stores supplied the change in appearance, and theme restaurants were the new entertainment.

"Alberto's Ristorante & Sports Bar" the sign said. The large script letters were burnt into wood, matching the upscale mahogany facade of the entrance.

So far so good – no flashing lights, Danny thought.

Danny opened the front door using its ornate brass handle. He took note of the inlaid, etched glass both in the solid oak door and in the vestibule. As each facet of Alberto's materialized, it assuaged his anxiety of walking into a dive.

It was 3 p.m., and there was a feeling of energy in the air, not only for tonight's big Yankee/Red Sox game, but also for the preparation of the evening meal.

The bar was oversized for a restaurant. *Probably the same one that girls had danced on at one time*, Danny thought. Big screen TV's could be seen from any angle. Danny noted that all of the servers were women in mid-thigh, light khaki skirts, and white sleeveless blouses – all attractive and not obscene. There were booths and plenty of room at the bar to enjoy a meal as opposed to eating in the dining room. Danny looked into the main room and noted how the tables were neatly adorned in white linen with a small vase of freshly cut flowers on each one. He felt the arrangement to see if they were real, which was a habit of his. A commotion at the bar drew his attention to the bartender. She had long, thick blonde hair, tied in a pony tail with two knots. Danny took two steps toward the bar, but was stopped short by a rapidly approaching, spry, older man. He was waving his arm in a gesture of greeting.

"I'm Albert Balletta," he said.

"Hi I'm Danny Lopez." Their extended hands shook. Danny expected a smaller hand from someone, whom he towered over, but Albert's was about the same size, and his grip was strong.

Still grasping Danny's hand, Albert asked. "Were you that fighter in the Golden Gloves that knocked out Travis Smalls?" Before Danny could answer, he added. "Did you know that Smalls is fighting for the heavyweight title? How come *you* didn't turn pro?"

He seemed to already know, so no sense in trying to do a dance around this question.

"Yeah that's me alright." Danny shook his head.

Albert let go of his hand and added. "I was at that fight with my nephew and I said to him, that this kid was going to be pound for pound the best someday. What happened?"

"I became the best pound for pound history teacher instead."

Albert gave Danny a hard, playful slap on the shoulder and burst out with the most infectious laughter Danny had ever heard. Danny could not keep from laughing along with Albert; even though he didn't think what he said was *that* funny. In between his outburst Albert said, "most people I slap like that usually fall over," he continued to laugh. Danny didn't interrupt and let him finish.

"And now before I show you around, I want you to meet Gino. He will handle the rough stuff. *Your* job is to smooth over the high paying customers. The bar area is your responsibility; the dining room is hardly ever a problem. Wear a suit and a tie, no sports jackets, dress just like you are now. You'll get two hundred dollars a night. Before you leave, stop by at my office to fill out a tax form; got to keep my accountant happy. This is not an off-the-books job, I'm strictly legitimate."

"I understand and I like it that way."

"Well, you'll be my first non-cop in this job. I guess you know you're hired; and you can start tonight." They shook hands again.

"GINO!" Albert called out.

From out of the kitchen came what Danny could only explain as a walking barrel.

"If you ever need to find him, look in the kitchen first," said Albert.

Gino was thirty-five years old, seven inches shorter and outweighed Danny by over seventy-five pounds.

As soon as he saw Danny standing with Albert, he picked up the pace, as much as his body could.

"Man I heard you were coming here. I saw you fight in the 'Gloves,' I was there, man, I love boxing." He then took up a fighter's stance and swung his arms around his belly.

He's probably very strong and as long as he is moving forward, his momentum should carry him through any trouble, Danny thought. *And if he took a step backwards, he would probably continue in that direction, too, until he struck something.*

Gino shook Danny's hand with both of his, and then was motioned off by Albert. Gino went back to the kitchen.

"He's my nephew, what can I say."

"He seems genuine Albert, I'm sure he does a good job. And another thing, you don't have to worry about his loyalty."

Albert paused for a moment and looked Danny in the eyes, then nodded his head in approval. He showed him around by pointing out each section. The main dining room, huge sports bar and Gino's kitchen.

A short pause in the conversation was broken when Danny asked, "Who's 'Renée Zellweger' behind the bar?"

"That's Kristen. I know she looks good, but I hired for her bartending skills, and I'm getting my moneys worth. I have to tell you, I've seen a lot of guys trying to hit on her, but they all seem to bounce off."

"Thanks for the heads-up. Bouncing off of the ropes is my specialty."

"Don't say I didn't warn you," said Albert as he walked away. "Oh," he added, "don't forget to circulate – don't stand in one place, be loose. You'll do fine, Champ."

"Thanks, Albert."

∾

Danny walked toward the bar - his final destination was set at Kristen, but his path was not in a straight line. Kristen kept her head down as she saw Danny approaching in a zigzag manner.

He's "accidentally" coming toward me. Who does he think he's kidding?

Besides being huge, the pure mahogany bar was deep; a leftover feature used for accommodating the dancers. Now it served a dual purpose of having dinner and watching the local sports event. After maneuvering a path not unlike a ship trying to avoid being torpedoed, Danny, at last, arrived at the bar.

Kristen did not look up from organizing the clean glasses.

Danny stood opposite her, and spoke over her lowered head, "Hi I'm Danny, and I've been hired to protect you."

Kristen looked up, "So you're the new 'super hero.' Do I look frail and weak to you? If I want protection, I'll call Gino. Why don't you find some corner to direct traffic and then go home and protect your wife with your gun."

Danny stood for a moment, taking in what she had just told him, and her green eyes, which had melted their way into his heart.

"Okay, I'm going to walk back over there." Danny pointed across the room. "And then I'm coming back. For the record, I don't know the first thing about directing traffic, I don't need a gun, and I don't have a wife that needs protecting. In fact, I don't have a wife."

Danny turned his back to the bar, walked to the street

entrance and then walked back to Kristen; this time in a straight line.

"Now let me say this," he began. "I apologize for the 'protection' remark and I apologize in advance for any other stupid remark that I hope I don't say. My name is Danny Lopez and I teach history at a high school out on Long Island." He held out his hand.

He seems honest enough and those dimples are awfully cute. Why not? she thought.

Kristen's strong hand attached to a slim wrist was extended to Danny's.

The touch of her hand gave Danny a feeling that he had not yet experienced. *If there was such a thing as love at first site, could this be love at first touch?* Danny thought. *Did my heart just skip a beat? Am I one of those cartoon characters, where, at this moment, little red hearts are spewing above my head?*

Danny came down to earth.

"Is there something wrong?" Kristen asked.

"No, not at all, but I didn't get *your* name."

"I'm Kristen Marks. And you don't look like a *Lopez*."

"So tell me, how should a 'Lopez' look?"

"Well I'll tell you one thing, there wouldn't be the map of Ireland printed across his face."

"Maybe I was adopted."

"Lucky you," she quickly responded.

"How do you mean that?" Danny asked.

"That would be too much information. I hardly know you."

"Well you see, Kristen, that's what this is all about. I greet you, I meet you, I ask you to go for coffee, and then dinner and then who knows what? Or you tell me to f-off – end of story. Since I haven't heard to the contrary, I think I'm doing pretty good."

Kristen turned her head slightly to the side, as if she didn't believe what she just heard, and then let out a giggle coinciding with her twinkling eyes. Danny loved it, it was infectious, and this time Danny's follow up laughter was genuine.

"At four o'clock the staff usually eats. That's fifteen minutes from now. So as soon as I'm done setting up these glasses, for tonight, we can have dinner right here at this beautiful mahogany table." Kristen said, suprising Danny.

Oscar delivered the scallops and fettuccine to the bar; he then paused and looked at Danny.

"You're Danny Lopez, the fighter?" Oscar asked.

"Not anymore, I'm here to talk people *out* of violence."

Oscar held out his hand and Danny shook it.

"Thank you Champ, it's nice to meet you." Oscar then walked away.

"I never saw Oscar act that way. I thought you said that you were a teacher?" Kristen asked.

"I am. Oscar was referring to when I was a kid and did some boxing."

"He said 'Champ,' Danny. That means there was more to it than 'a couple of boxing matches.' Wouldn't you say that?"

"I say these scallops are tasty and the fettuccine is the best I've ever had. But let me ask *you* a question. What size are you?"

"What! Why do you want to know?"

"It's harmless, really, and I can explain it at another time."

"I've never been asked that in my entire life and I don't know why I'm even telling you this." Kristen tentatively answered, "I'm size two."

"And I won the Golden Gloves when I was a young man." Danny offered in return.

A parade of cooks came from the kitchen all eager to shake Danny's hand, followed by the three male bartenders who worked with Kristen. When Danny spoke in Spanish to the cooks, Kristen gave Danny her "surprise smile," where the tip of her tongue was held between her front teeth. She did this to keep from going into the all out giggle. Danny loved it.

Besides her size, Kristen revealed that she taught math at Edmund Hall High School in Queens.

❧ CHAPTER EIGHTEEN ❧

Everyone was already at the house in Queens for this Sunday's dinner. As usual Danny arrived last.

Tito and Mario were in the den getting ready for the third Yankee/Red Sox game.

"We'll take 'em today, two out of three ain't bad." Mario said. He motioned to Danny to take a seat on the sofa. Marisol brought him a coke in a glass with a doily.

"Got your little doily to put under your cuppy, little boy?" Tito kidded Danny.

Both Tito and Mario drank from a can or bottle. Danny always used a glass.

"Keep it up and I'll spank the both of you," scolded Marisol.

"You let me know if they're still picking on you," Marisol said to Danny.

"Yes Mommy," Danny replied in a little boys voice.

She mockingly glared and smiled at Tito and Mario, before returning to the kitchen.

"So how's it going at the restaurant, Bro?" Tito asked.

"Good, good, real good." He answered with a bland look on his face.

There was unusual silence until Mario spoke.

"You okay Danny?"

"I'm fine, man, really. Just a little tired from the new job."

Quiet reigned again.

This time Tito spoke. "You seem different, Danny."

Danny could no longer contain his huge grin.

And both Tito and Mario knew immediately.

Mario yelled into the kitchen. "Hey Mom, Danny's got himself an *amorcita*.

Hector came out from the kitchen with a sample of today's meal.

"What's going on?" He asked..

Before Hector could get his answer, Marisol, Maria, Trisha and Colleen, all emerged from the kitchen and surrounded Danny.

"It's no big deal," Danny said.

"I met this girl at the restaurant, she's a teacher like I am and that's about it."

"That's about it he says. He *never* looked this way. Oh yeah, what is she, size one?" Mario asked.

"No she's not, wise guy. She's size two. And if it all works out, you'll meet her in due time."

"That's it!" Marisol ordered. "Everyone back to the kitchen, we have some work to do before dinner. *And* leave Danny alone."

The meeting broke up, leaving only the men in the den.

After a short lull Tito spoke. "She must be someone

special, Danny. These things usually happen out of the blue. So if it works out, all the best Bro."

They all raised their bottles and cans and Danny his glass for a toast well made.

❧ CHAPTER NINETEEN ❧

Danny and Kristen both worked on Sunday nights and were off on Mondays and Tuesdays. After dinner with his family, he drove Tito's black 2005 Jeep Liberty through the midtown tunnel and over to Alberto's; parking, close by, in a "free" space thanks to Tito's connections. Tito's wife Trisha, wanted a larger vehicle, and instead of trading it in, Tito offered it to Danny. The Liberty was five years old and looked as if it had just been driven out of the showroom.

"I'll be able to buy it from you with the money I get from working at the restaurant." He had said.

"Take your time Bro." Tito had responded.

Danny knew that he and Trisha would give it to him if he had shown any signs of hardship. In the meantime, he insisted that he pay Tito for the auto insurance.

He saw Kristen coming down the block from the opposite direction. He waited and held open the oversized front door.

"Thank you, kind sir. So how was dinner?" Kristen asked.

"Always a good time, they make me feel special, always have." Danny answered, and at the same time thinking how she was the main topic following the main course.

"That's really nice Danny. You're so lucky to have been born into such a great family."

"I wasn't. They picked me. That's when the lucky part began. I was adopted."

Kristen's eyes became moist as she remembered. "I'm sorry that when I first met you, and you told me that *maybe* you were adopted, and I said, 'lucky you.' It was mean and angry of me. I didn't know you then, but that was no excuse to put my baggage on you."

"Could we have dinner in a booth instead of at the bar?" Danny asked.

"Sure Danny, that's okay with me."

Danny sat opposite her in the booth and placed his hand on top of hers.

"From the first time I laid eyes on you, I felt a connection. Even when you didn't want any part of me, I knew there was no way that I would give up. And now I can only explain it as chemistry. So if there's something that you want to tell me, I'm a good listener." Danny waited for a response.

"You…you tell me your story first, Danny."

"Okay, that's easy. When I was six years old, both of my parents died in an auto accident. I was put into foster homes, one worse than the other, until one day I got lucky and I found the Lopez family, and the good part is that they found me too. It was mutual" Danny stopped talking. "And as you can see it's also emotional for me."

Kristen's hands were on her cheeks to catch the tears flowing freely around her finger tips.

"I've done well." Danny continued, "And I look to do better. Now it's your turn."

"I think you just made a hard time sound easy. I'm afraid my story is what happens when you *don't* get lucky. Like you, I did get my education, but unlike you, for the most part, my relationships have sucked. Oh and another thing, I'm not a champ of anything." Kristen removed her hands from her face and a smile appeared.

She continued. "I got my name from Saint Mark's Church. *Someone* left me there as an infant. I was given the name Mary Kathryn Marks. I chose to be called Kristen when I was around eight, and had my name legally changed when I was nineteen. So, Danny, as a math teacher I would have to say, the sum result is that I don't really have anyone."

"Well you have me, Kristen. You have me," he repeated. "You've overcome a lot more then I have. I got to be called 'champ,' because I knocked someone out, but you knocked me over, so I guess you're the *new* champ."

Kristen put her tongue between her teeth and let a little giggle slip out.

They spent Monday and Tuesday holding hands and walking the City; going to dinner other than at Alberto's, and driving Kristen to her rented apartment in Queens, where she would serve Danny coffee before he returned to Long Island.

After giving Danny coffee to keep him awake for his drive home, they stood in her doorway. She looked up at him as he took her by the shoulders and drew her in. Her perky breasts felt good against his thin shirt and her mouth generated an urge of more to come, until she broke it off and said goodnight for a second time.

∾

Wednesday night for Danny and Kristen began in the same way as other work days; with dinner together before starting their shifts.

The sports bar was becoming a big draw and it was the food that drew them in; all because Albert had won over a top chef to head up his kitchen. The diners were arriving earlier, and then would adjourn to the bar and mingle with the already overflow crowd. After-dinner-drinks replaced dessert for the dinner patrons while beer remained the staple for the sports enthusiasts. Kristen had to keep a close watch on indulgence, and Danny kept one eye on any person who might be "stepping over the line" with Kristen.

During a lull in her services, Danny moved to an empty space at the bar.

"How's it going?" Danny asked.

"You mean how am I doing with the guys hitting on me? I'm doing fine, but you're going to have to, *please*, raise the bar of your tolerance level to mine." She begged. "I'm flattered, but remember that I did this before I met you. I can handle it."

"I'll try; it's just that......." Danny was interrupted.

"I know Danny and I can't tell you how much I appreciate it. If someone gets out of hand, I'll let you know." She raised her eyebrows and nodded her head for his approval.

"Okay." Danny acknowledged.

∾

The commotion came before the dinner customers and before the bar crowd had built up for the evening.

Through the front door came huge bodies dressed all in black.

"MAKE WAY FOR THE NEXT CHAMP! THAT'S RIGHT, THE NEXT HEAVYWEIGHT CHAMPION OF THE WORLD!"

There were four of them creating a wedge for Travis Smalls who was dressed in a white silk suit, and black open neck shirt.

Albert came out from the back office. "What the hell is going on?"

Danny held up his hand to Albert. Travis Small was yet to see Danny. As he broke through his entourage, he came face to face with his old adversary.

"Hello Travis." Danny said without extending his hand. He could hardly hear his own voice above the din that was being created by Travis' "men in waiting."

"Man you're the last one I would think of to be standing in front of me," said Travis who had trouble speaking above the shouting. He turned to one of them. "Big Dog, tell them to shut the fuck up." Big Dog did as he was told. There was immediate obedience.

"I sent a card." Travis said.

"I know you did, I thought that was classy of you." Danny responded,

Travis moved away from the bar activity and Danny went with him.

"It wasn't class what I said to you. I tried to tell you that with the card, because I wasn't man enough to look you up and tell that to your face. I was a young punk kid, and you handed this punk what he deserved. I hope you have forgiven me."

"I forgave you when I knocked you out." Danny smiled.

Travis stared at him for a second, and then broke out in a big grin.

Danny held out his arms and they both embraced. "Something that we didn't do that night; you were laying on your back and I figured it just wouldn't look right." Danny quipped, and Travis' grin grew larger. Danny added. "On Saturday night, you take it to him, and bring the title back to the U.S.A., Champ."

Travis turned to Big Dog and said. "I'm going to tell you who the real champ is."

Immediately, Big Dog and the rest of his men started chanting, "YOU'RE THE REAL CHAMP! YOU'RE THE REAL CHAMP!"

Travis gave Big Dog a cold stare and said, "Shut them up!"

Big Dog did as he was told.

Standing in front of the bar, with Kristen on the other side, Travis raised Danny's hand and said, "This is the real champion! He is the only man to beat me and the only man to ever put me on my ass. Danny Lopez is the reason that I will bring the championship home this Friday. Not only is he a better fighter, he showed me how a better man should behave."

The bar crowd cheered and Albert went back to his office.

After they had their sodas, Travis left as he had entered, with the chanting of, CHAMP! CHAMP! CHAMP!

The diners started to gather at the bar, and all that Travis brought with him this night was soon forgotten.

Danny smiled at Kristen who smiled back. This would be their only contact until it was time to pack up for the evening.

The routine remained the same. He drove her home, had his coffee, and then went back to Long Island.

❧ CHAPTER TWENTY ❧

On Thursday afternoon a truck jack-knifed on the Long Island Expressway, and ended up on its side; blocking two of the three West bound lanes. This caused Danny to be unusually late.

When he came through the entrance of Alberto's his first concern was to always seek out Kristen. He was surprised to find a police officer blocking his view.

"Excuse me Sergeant, but aren't you away from your jurisdiction, precinct or whatever?" Danny asked.

"This place is actually close to the border of two precincts and three blocks from my 'jurisdiction' as you put it. However, as far as you're concerned, sonny, it's none of your business," replied the Sergeant.

Kristen's smile was getting wider and wider.

Pretty soon that giggle is going to kick in, Danny thought.

"I guess you don't recognize me, tough guy, I *just* happen to be a Golden Gloves Champion, *and* a knockout artist." Danny said, in a haughty way.

"Well B.F.D.(big fucking deal), I'll cuff you, and then we'll see how good you are at playing Houdini as opposed to playing boxer." He turned to Kristen, "Sorry for the language. Oh, and by the way," he added, pointing to Kristen, "the only knockout I see here is her."

"So you want to play tough?" Danny answered. "If you use your cuffs on me, I'll tell Mom, and she'll have you standing in the corner."

"You don't fight fair." Tito said in a defeated voice.

They didn't let the banter go on any further and ended it with a hug and pat on the back.

"What are you doing here?" Danny asked.

"I'm just checking out where my younger brother is working, that's all." Tito answered.

"Are you sure that's all you're checking out, Bro?" Danny said while turning to Kristen, who was tee hee'ing with the tip of her tongue between her front teeth.

"As you already know, this is my brother, Tito." Kristen gave a short wave from behind the bar and Tito waved back.

Tito looked at Danny and Kristen, and even *his* heart skipped a beat for them.

Kristen had served Tito a coke, and as he reached for it, she noticed his pink bracelet. Her eyes instinctively shifted to Danny and she saw a wisp of pink showing from under his white cuff. Before this time she had not thought to look for one.

When Tito walked into Alberto's, it caused a stir, but not one that would bring about panic. Everyone who worked there knew, that except for Danny, the security of Alberto's was usually handled by moonlighting policemen. And since the changeover from strip club, to what is considered in the NYPD's Integrity Monitoring File, as a legitimate establishment, it was removed from the "List."

Tito went right up to Kristen, who had her back to the bar, and had asked, "Can I have a coke, Kristen?" His voice made her jump.

The uniform and fact they he knew her name, startled her, but when she read his name tag, "Lopez," she was relieved.

"How did you know enough to use my name?"

"Although Danny really didn't describe you, no one else behind the bar seemed to be his type. They're all too heavy."

That remark had started the giggle, only for it to intensify after Danny walked in.

"Well I gotta go, Bro. No bad guys here; hasn't been for some time. And besides that, we usually have a cop working here. It's like the place is an auxiliary police booth. Will we see you this Sunday?"

"Yeah, late as usual, but I'll be there."

"Good," Tito turned toward Kristen. "He's me and my brother Mario's target and we practice on him quite a lot. And then the rest of the family, including my wife, comes to his defense. It's the same story every Sunday, and we never get tired of it. It's not much fun when he can't make it. See you Sunday, Danny."

They hugged, did the pat on the back, and then Tito left, but not before acknowledging Kristen. "You're everything I expected without Danny saying anything about you. Nice meeting you."

They reached over the bar to hug around the neck, and then he was gone.

"Who's the cop?" Albert had walked over from the kitchen entrance.

"He's my brother." Danny answered.

"That's good to hear because we haven't much to do with the legal stuff since I got rid of the dancers and all their other activity." Albert rolled his eyes and shook his head. "We don't make as much money as with the girls, but there's no trouble either; especially trying to conform to the less than 40 per cent square footage of adult entertainment law that the mayor had championed. Now we have a new mayor and I have a different business – me and the City are probably both better off. And I can live with less money. Between the girls, the City Inspectors, *and* the lawyers, I'm probably netting more now." He nodded his head and went back to his office, but not before looking into the kitchen, again.

"He seems very nervous," said Danny.

"Every Saturday night, around midnight, they come to collect their money for the linen service." Kristen answered.

"Who's 'they' and why does paying for linen service make him nervous?" Danny asked.

"The 'they' might be 'wise guys,' or at least they act like you see them in the movies."

∾

Danny's routine of bringing Kristen to her apartment continued for Thursday night and again on Friday. Friday had been especially crowded, which changed Albert's mood; he now had more than enough to pay the linen extorters.

He was charged twice the going market for linen service which included the "benefit to run his business without problems." *At least I'm using linens, with the strip club I paid for something I never got.* Albert thought.

Both the dining room and the bar were filled to capacity with non-stop activity.

The crowd stayed late and Kristen was glad that Danny could take her home. She took off her shoes in the car, brought the seat back, and put her feet up on the dashboard; offering a view of her legs, beyond what her khaki skirt allowed. Danny's eyes took it all in.

"There were times tonight when I didn't know if I gave the right drink to the right person. I'll say one thing, they all seemed very happy."

Danny could hardly keep his eyes open.

"Are you okay?" she asked.

"I feel like I just went about fifty rounds. I think it's more of my inactivity that got me this way. Once in a while Gino would come by, from the kitchen of course, and he broke the monotony."

The walk up the stairs to the second floor apartment drained what little strength they had left. As Kristen inserted her key in the door, it slipped out and she stumbled in picking it up. Danny caught her and held her around the waist; bringing her up to him, he kissed her. Kristen's arms went instinctively around his neck and then she slowly lowered them, turned, and opened the door.

Danny drank his coffee, and Kristen for a change, had coffee instead of tea. "I need the caffeine, and believe me, it won't keep me awake."

They sat close to each other on stools, set up at the room divider; it separated the small kitchen area from the combination living room dining room.

"I noticed your bother was wearing a pink bracelet" Kristen pause to sip her coffee. "I noticed, for the first time, yesterday, that you are wearing one too. Is there any significance to it?"

"Yes," Danny answered softly. "Our Mother had a scare, and from that moment on, our whole family have been supporters."

Kristen put both of her hands on Danny's. "I have something to tell you, actually two things to tell you, and I don't know which one to tell you first." Her lips began to quiver, something that Danny had never seen before.

"I shouldn't tell you this first, but if my dream is shattered, then at least, I would have once had a dream." Kristen paused to wipe away tears from both eyes. "I've fallen in love with you, I wouldn't want a life without you in it."

Danny was confused

"I love you, Kristen. I've loved you, maybe, from the first time I saw you. You're all I think about when you're not with me."

They had turned from the divider and were facing each other. He put his hand on her shoulders to draw her in, and she put her hand on his chest.

"There's something wrong, isn't there?" said Danny. "Please tell me what it is?"

There was very little space between their faces.

"I'm a cancer survivor, Danny. I got breast cancer when I was eighteen. I was a phenomenon; no one gets breast cancer at eighteen. The medical scientists paid me for their research, and I used the money to pay for my education and to change my name."

Danny knew not to interrupt.

"I....don't...." Kristen was breathing heavily. Danny took hold of her shoulders, again.

"They took...they had to remove one of my breasts."

There I've said it for the first time; oh my god I just want to die.

"How could anybody love me like this?"

Danny was blinking back tears. "That's part of who you are now, and I love you Kristen Marks. I love the soul of your life, which has become part of me."

Danny picked her up off of the stool and carried her into her bedroom. As he looked into her eyes, he began to undo the buttons of her white blouse. She stopped him.

"Please, please," Danny pleaded.

Kristen turned away from him and placed his hands around her waist.

"Okay," she said.

He undid the buttons and let the blouse fall to the floor. As he undid the bra clasps from behind, Kristen brought her hands up to her breasts. When the bra was undone, she lifted it away. Danny saw the prosthesis in the right cup. Before Danny could bring his hands around front, she turned and faced him. Danny's hands touched her.

He looked into her glistening eyes and said. "*Como nadie no podra quererte?*"

"What did you just say?" Kristen asked.

"I said, how could anyone *not* love you."

Kristen could no longer blink back her tears.

"You are so beautiful inside and out, please stay with me forever," said Danny.

Overwhelmed with their emotions, they embraced and wept, unabashedly.

"I don't want to drive home tonight," he said

"I don't want you to," she replied and added, "I loved the way it sounded in Spanish."

Kristen's bed was a single, but it didn't matter; exhausted, they slept the night, clinging to each other.

∽

The morning sun opened the first day in their new life.

"Thank you for being gentle," Kristen said.

"Thank you for being rough," Danny replied.

Kristen hit him with her pillow. Danny grabbed the pillow which was about to strike again and his momentum carried him on top of her; her hands along with Danny's were holding the pillow over her head. She instinctively opened her legs allowing Danny to enter her once again. This time they were energized from a good night sleep, and their desires were driven at a hungry pace.

As Danny lay back, he rolled over; almost falling out of the small bed. Kristen grabbed at his arm, but Danny had all ready righted himself.

Danny showered first, while Kristen was washing and drying his underwear and socks.

When Kristen came out of the shower, she found Danny examining her prosthesis.

"Don't I have *any* privacy?" she exclaimed.

Danny ignored her. "It's a perfect match; skin color, including the nipple." Danny noted.

"I'm not going to ask you how you know all of this, because I don't want to play little miss innocent in your little game. It's not an accident that the boobs match. It was custom made and I can wear it with or without a bra, depending on how tight a top I have on. It fits perfectly into my bras including my bikini top. Now you have it all. And stop kneading my breast. Please!"

"It feels just like your other one."

"I know you're trying to get me to say, how did you come by that conclusion? But I'm not going to go there. *How sweet of him to say 'your other one' instead of your 'real one,'* she thought. The cost was a throw in by the study group, on top of the money."

Before going over to Alberto's, they took a detour to Danny's place on Long Island so that he could pack a suitcase for his sleepovers.

CHAPTER TWENTY-ONE

Kristen and Danny walked into Alberto's, and only released their hands as they entered the doorway.

Albert waved hello to them. He seemed unusually happy for a Saturday, according to Kristen.

"I guess he has the money for them," she said.

Except for Travis Smalls fighting for the heavyweight title, the night was uneventful.

At twelve O'clock they came through the door, there were three of them. *Kristen was right, they looked to be playing parts from The Godfather Movie,* Danny thought. Except they weren't playing, not the way they flung open the door. One of them went in a straight line to the back office and the other two went to the bar. The short fat man sought out the first bartender who could serve him, but the thick necked muscular one went directly to Kristen. He elbowed a patron to get the spot in front of her. She held up her hand to Danny as she saw him make a move toward the bar. He didn't stop and took up a position next to "muscles."

"Nice day today, Yanks won." Danny said to him.

"What the fuck are you, a fucking sportscaster?" He answered.

Kristen rolled her eyes as she could imagine those beautiful muscles of Danny rippling under his shirt. She pleaded with her eyes to him.

"Hey Frankie, don't you know who he is? He's a fucking Golden Gloves Champion." The short fat man waddled over with a drink in one hand and the other held out for Danny to shake. Kristen looked relieved.

"Hi, I'm Vinny, I saw you fight that night – great fight. Travis Smalls is fighting tonight. Who do ya think will win?"

"Smalls will bury him." Danny replied.

While Danny was talking to Vinny, Frankie was standing and fuming.

Kristen had purposely changed positions with another bartender and was serving a crowd, four deep.

The new bartender asked Frankie, "What would you like to drink?"

"Fuck you," Frankie answered.

The bartender shrugged and asked Vinny if *he* wanted another drink.

Danny asked Frankie, "I never heard of the 'fuck you drink,' but if you can tell us what's in it, I'm sure we can have it for you on your next visit."

Frankie responded with, "Who the fuck do you…..?" but was stopped short when Sam strutted out of the back office and signaled them to leave. Sam was a "made man" in the mob, and Frankie and Vinny were just "associates" on the organization chart. They did and moved as he said, without any questions.

"Why did you antagonize him, was it because of me? Because I told you that I can take care of guys like him. Now I'm worried for you." Kristen pleaded.

"Don't worry, their time has past. Did you see how they puppy dogged it out of here when their boss was ready to go? If it makes you feel any better, next week I won't push him."

Danny didn't answer her question – but she knew that he did it because of her, and was both proud and upset at the same time.

The rest of the evening went without incident and Kristen and Danny went home together.

❧ CHAPTER TWENTY-TWO ❧

They took Kristen's BMW to the Lopez house on Sunday.

"A BMW!" Danny had originally exclaimed.

"Don't get overly excited," she had said, "it's ten years old. I always wanted one, and this is what I could afford."

As they pulled into the driveway, Danny was relating to Kristen, the first time that he was driven here by Hector.

Kristen became very emotional. "Great, I'm going to meet your family for the first time, and all they're going to remember is my red nose."

"It's not that red; by the time we get inside, it'll be fine."

Kristen was wearing an over the knee, slim brown skirt and a matching jacket with a cream colored blouse. Danny had on a three button shirt and dress pants. Kristen called it his "bully" shirt, because it showed off his muscles.

Tito was waiting at the front door.

Hug after hug assured Kristen that Danny was loved and that she was wanted; including a very special one, she thought, given to her by Marisol. The banter that she witnessed between Danny and Tito in Alberto's was magnified many times over.

After dinner, as usual, the men went to the den, but Danny observed Marisol and Kristen going upstairs. *Probably showing her his old room*, he thought.

"What do think of Smalls knocking out that Russian guy for the World Championship?" Tito asked Danny.

"He visited the restaurant the other night and I wished him luck."

"He did?" exclaimed Mario.

"He said he was sorry about the way he acted at the Gloves. What was it, about ten years ago? Anyway I'm glad he won."

"Ever think how it could have been if you had turned pro Danny?" Mario asked.

Hector who had been dosing off, became alert for the answer.

"Never have. I told Mom that I just wanted to win the Golden Gloves Open, and that's what I meant. And besides that, I wouldn't have met Kristen. You see it all works out for the best."

Hector went back to dosing off.

When Marisol and Kristen came back downstairs, it was obvious to him that they had both been crying. They stayed in the den with the men and didn't immediately return to the kitchen until they had recovered. Danny felt that he was the only one in the den who noticed.

Dessert was served and then there was the usual mingling between the den, dining room and kitchen. Kristen stayed with Danny in the Den.

"So what were you and Mom talking about, upstairs?" Danny asked.

She leaned over on the couch and whispered in his ear. "Girl stuff, I'll tell you later."

Kristen stayed with Danny, until it was time to do the dishes.

"I thought that's what we got the dishwasher for," said Mario.

"They still have to be wiped off, stacked and then dried, but of course if you have a better way, you can show us." Mario's wife Colleen called from the kitchen.

"I'm sorry I can't," he called back. "The Red Sox are winning and I have to stay in my lucky seat for the Yanks."

After dessert and after the game, the house cleared out. But not without great fanfare directed toward Kristen. For a change, Danny was the last to leave.

"*Jou* found a nice girl Danny, I'm very happy for *jou*," said Hector.

Kristen held Hector's hands and said, "Danny told me all about what you and Marisol did to get him."

"Please call us Mom and Dad," Marisol injected.

"You know that I have never called anyone that, *ever*."

"Well that streak ends right now," said Marisol

Kristen paused before she spoke. "Thank you Mom and thank you Dad for showing Danny your love by opening up your arms to him and now those strong arms of his embrace me. I know that Danny loves you both with all of his heart, and I thank God for that heart."

Hector, Marisol, Danny and Kristen were all wiping their eyes.

Laughing as she dabbed her eyes with a Kleenex, Marisol said, "I guess we all have the emotional Lopez gene, that's what makes us a family, including you, Kristen."

On the way home, Kristen spoke about her conversation with Danny's mother.

"Thank you for telling your mother."

"I knew that it would be good if she knew. And I told her not to tell anyone else," said Danny.

"She was wonderful. I can't go into our conversation anymore than that, without crying; not tears of sadness, but of closure."

"Then don't, and leave it be."

❦ CHAPTER TWENTY-THREE ❦

Mario had Tuesday off, and volunteered the use of his pickup truck, so that he and Danny could bring a double mattress from Macy's warehouse annex to Kristen's apartment; her bed frame was adaptable. Mario insisted that he come along and help, and not just loan Danny his truck; together they carried the mattress up to Kristen's apartment.

From the Golden Gloves Championship fight on, Mario grasped at any opportunity to make up for his angry years. Danny would put up a tepid refusal, but then would "give in" and let Mario do what he felt he had to do.

The rest of the week was business as usual at Alberto's, except for Friday. This is when a water main burst and the City shut down Alberto's block. The street was closed to vehicular traffic and jammed with all varieties of construction apparatus; making it difficult for even the pedestrians to get through. The result was a drop off of business on a big receipt day, causing Albert to come up short for Saturday night's collection.

By Saturday morning, the water main was fixed and

the customers had returned for the afternoon and evening sessions.

"He's so jittery, I feel so sorry for him," said Kristen as she wiped the bar down.

"I know what you mean. I'm avoiding eye contact and staying away from the path to the office." Danny replied.

"On that note," pleaded Kristen. "Please promise to stay away from *me* tonight *too*. Let them do their business and leave. I know you aren't afraid of him, (she purposely didn't use his name) but I'm sure he has a gun, and that makes *me* scared. Please do this for me," she pleaded, again.

"Okay, okay, I'll stay away. In fact I'll go into the kitchen and keep Gino company."

Kristen smiled, but did not believe him.

Twelve o'clock came and so did the collectors. Frankie went directly over to Kristen, Sam went to the office, Vinny went to the far end of the bar, and Danny went into the kitchen.

Gino was eating a large plate of meatballs as Danny walked in. Danny greeted him by holding up his hand and Gino returned the acknowledgement by holding up a fork with a meatball; it was in suspended animation before entering his mouth. Danny smiled to himself and turned to look out at Kristen through the narrow rectangular window that ran along the top of the kitchen door.

Gino went back to his meatballs, but when he went to put the fork into his mouth, again, he stopped short. Loud shouting was coming through the wall just behind his private dining area. Albert's office was on the other side and this worried him. He listened intently, and heard the fierce tone of Sam's voice. He was angry and something was being slammed. Gino knew what Sam represented, but Albert was more of a father to him than an uncle. He strode to the door and couldn't stop his momentum before bumping into Danny.

"What's the matter?" Danny asked.

"I...I think my uncle's in trouble."

Danny paused for a moment, thinking back to when *he* stuttered.

"Let me handle it," said Danny. "I'm not involved like you. I haven't got that whole Italian vendetta intrigue thing going. You stay here and watch Kristen to make sure that jerk doesn't step over the line."

"Sure, sure, I can do that Danny. I won't let anything happen to Kristen."

Gino was both happy to protect Danny's girlfriend, and not to be part of whatever was going on in the office.

When Danny opened the door and stepped in, Albert was more startled than Sam.

"What the fuck do you want?" said Sam.

"I thought you would like a cup of coffee from the kitchen?" Danny asked. *What's with the anger with these guys?*

Sam looked at him as if Danny had just spoken another language. Albert shook his head.

"Danny," Albert spoke. "This is not a good time. I'll call you if we want something from the kitchen." Albert spoke in a calm steady voice.

"Danny?" said Sam. "Are you the adopted son of that washed up *spic* boxer, the son who didn't have the guts to turn pro?" He was standing in front of Albert's desk and looking over his shoulder at Danny.

Danny grabbed hold of his collar at the back of his neck, and flung him across the room. Sam slid through a pile of ledgers and ended up with his head in an empty bookshelf. Danny saw the gun come out and kicked it out of his hand.

His presence in the room was felt before Danny saw any movement. Frankie was stalled at the doorway, wondering where Sam was. When he saw Sam on the floor, he drew his gun. But before Danny could move, Gino came bounding into Frankie knocking the gun out of his hand and landing him onto the floor next to Sam.

"Pick those up and get the hell out" said Danny pointing to the hand guns. "And next time, don't bring them in here or I'll call the law and you will be doing time. And for the record, *asshole*, my Father didn't have to be a world champion to be loved and respected. That's something you'll never know about, you piece of shit."

Frankie looked to say something, but was stopped by Danny's loud booming voice. "Don't you do or say anything, because I would like nothing better then to wipe up the floor with you."

As they left, Albert called out. "You tell the Stanuto's that they *know* I'm good for the money. I'll have it all for them next week." They made no response.

Albert motioned to Gino that he could go back to his kitchen. He thanked him for what he did. Gino was proud.

"Danny, Danny, Danny," said Albert. "These are the scum of the earth. They wouldn't hesitate to kill you while you were sitting in church. Until I can calm them down, and that's, *if* I could calm them down, you're going to have to disappear for a while. I think I can do this, but in the meantime, you can't be anywhere near where they could find you. My suggestion is to go on a vacation and leave not only the City, but the State. The Stanuto family looks for ways to show how tough they are. They're scum bags compared to the other crime families."

Danny tried to see if there was another way around the problem, "I don't see how I can leave, I . . ." He was interrupted.

"There's no other way around this problem. Please believe me." Albert said.

Danny quickly decided that it was Albert who was the expert here, and if he kept quiet, he just might learn something.

"The families are, now, so splintered, that I don't know if they even remember what family I belonged to. But, at one time, the crime family of Joey Sacco pulled a lot of weight. They know that I'm a 'made guy' like Sam, and I'm hoping this still means something. But if they get a wild hair up their ass, they'd *wack* you and me like they're impulse shopping. I can't take that chance with *you*."

"I'm overwhelmed with information," Danny said. "You say that I need to get away and take a vacation, but the reason that I'm working here is that I need the money to get me through the summer, *and* buy a car. Contrary to what people believe, teachers don't make that much."

Albert came out from behind his desk. He looked pensive. "I have something that might help. I've had it for a long time. It got me to be a 'made man,' and it's not something that I'm proud of." He walked toward one of the three file cabinets.

"Give me a hand."

Together they pushed one of the files away from the wall. Albert lifted the carpet where the file stood, and then piece by piece he removed the floor board. It was lying face up, and after three tries at spinning the dial, the safe door opened.

"Haven't opened this safe in years - many, many years."

Albert lifted out an attaché case.

"This money gets you out of here, but it comes with a burden."

He put the case on his desk, but did not open it.

"What I'm about to tell you, I never told nobody, no one, not even my family. And I'm sorry to put this on you, Danny, but I can't give this money to you without telling you its history. Back in 1963, me, and a wise guy named Joey Pinto went to Dallas from New Orleans. I was twenty years old and had driven Joey from New York. He was a funny guy and knew a lot of big shots everywhere; politicians, entertainers, sports guys, everybody. I was just a kid, and I looked up to him."

Albert took a deep breath.

"Anyway we get to Dallas – I was never to any of these places. Joey has me pull off of the road. I got as far off the road as possible without rolling down an embankment. I kept the Caddy's two driver's side wheels on solid ground while the passenger wheels were on grass. A storm drain was visible over my right shoulder and no sooner then I had stopped the car, Joey jumps out and goes right into it. I don't know how long it was before he came back, but when he did, he nonchalantly got into the car and said to no one in particular. 'The fucking ladder is missing the top step just as they said, so it won't be in my way when I lean forward; everything should go as planned. They wanted me to do it with some fucking clumsy Italian rifle, so they could pin it on some jerk. I told them that under twenty feet, I could hit a bird's beak with my twenty-five year old .44 Special, and that its long barrel was fitted for a silencer. I didn't give them a choice. They said okay and that they would get rid of any evidence of a .44 bullet.' Even on the trips from New York to New Orleans and then to Dallas, he never really spoke to me. It was a one sided conversation and I was there so it wouldn't be like he was talking to himself; which he really was. I listened and remembered, but I never asked about what we were doing."

Albert paused again and leaned harder on the attaché case.

"We stayed for three days in an apartment with someone who I thought was a cop, but he wasn't, he just had a uniform. We never went out; all of the meals were brought in by these 'dancers,' or at least that's what one of them told me she was. After a late breakfast on that third day, we go back to the same spot, but this time Joey gets out and opens the trunk. He pulls out a bag and runs into the hole. I waited for about thirty minutes, and when he comes back out, he has this wild eyed look on his face. Even his hair seemed electrified. He's ranting, 'I GOT HIM! I GOT HIM! I stood on that fucking iron ladder, while some *suit* stood and blocked the view from the sidewalk. The suit was there, and the storm drain wasn't sealed; everything was just as they said it would be. I did him, I did him,' he kept repeating. Who I asked? Because it looked like, for a change, he wanted me to ask. And then he told me. I was glad that he took a seat in the back, to 'stretch his legs,' I think he said. I do know that I *never* cried so hard without making a sound."

Albert's breathing seemed labored.

"Are you okay?" Danny asked.

Albert raised his hand and then continued.

"Every one knew that Joey was a crack shot and didn't have a conscience. Sirens were wailing all over the place as we headed out of Dallas. We drove for about fifty miles to a strip club in the middle of nowhere, and met up with some of the *goombas* I saw in New Orleans. We stayed for a couple days in some of the back rooms before I took Joey back to New York. While we stayed at the club, I listened to their conversation about there being three shooters; one on the sixth floor of the Book Depository, but on the opposite end of the building where they had the 'set up,' as they called it. We had a guy behind a picket fence on the, so called, Grassy Knoll, but the guy in the building wasn't one of us. It still hurts to say who we killed, but you *do* know, don't you?"

Danny, very slowly, nodded yes.

Albert opened the case.

"There should be twenty thousand dollars in here, all in twenties. I never counted it and I never even touched them. It's all yours Danny."

"I…" Danny started to say.

Albert interrupted him,

"To me, this money is polluted, but to you, you can make good use of it. Give it away if that makes you feel good, but you have a need for it now, so please take it from me. This was some of the money that Joey got and he gave me what he thought I deserved. He was ruthless, but he was honorable. I don't know who paid him and, as far as I know, nobody even knows he gave me anything. And I have to tell you one more thing, Joey was killed a couple of years ago, but I know it wasn't anyone of *us* that did it – not in the way he was killed.

He was a 'stand up guy,' a guy that could be counted on to keep his mouth shut."

Albert closed the attaché case and handed it to Danny.

"I'm sorry that you had to get mixed up in my dirty business. And I'm sorry that in ridding myself of this mess, I had to load in onto you. I don't think it would be fair, if you didn't know its background. It ain't a pretty story, and even though I could claim complete innocence, the fact is, that I did help. Do something good with this money, Danny. If nothing else, for a while, it will give you a way out of here. I should be able to straighten this mess out way before you run out of this dough."

Danny shook Albert's hand, in silence, while holding the attaché case in his left hand. They both knew that any further conversation was not necessary.

Danny walked out of the office and into the main bar area. The look on his face caused Kristen to be concerned.

"What's the matter Danny?" Kristen exclaimed as she stood behind the bar.

"It seems that I may have ruffled the feathers on the wrong bird. Back in the office, I came to Albert's defense, and because of that, he now says that my life might be in danger. I thought, no way, but Albert made me see another world and now I have to leave here for a while."

"Leave where?"

"Leave here, leave New York. I've only had the time it takes to walk from the office to here, but there is a Lopez cousin that I met at both of my brother's and sister's weddings. He lives in Albuquerque, New Mexico. That's the only thing that

I could come up with right now. Maybe when I have more time to think, I can come up with something better."

Kristen's hands came up from her sides and onto the bar for Danny to hold.

"You have to take me. I have no one but you."

"I can't do that. It'll be too dangerous and . . ." Danny was interrupted.

"If it's dangerous for me, it's dangerous for you too. And I'm not going to stay here alone, and *be* alone. What if they find out that we're connected? Please, Danny, please. I'll watch out for you as much as you will for me."

His hesitation was not long.

"Okay," he said. "Maybe Albert will straighten this out quickly and we'll be treating this as a short vacation."

"I have money in my account," said Kristen.

"We won't need it. I can explain later, but I think we better get started right away."

"What about Albert, doesn't he have to know about me?" She asked.

"He probably already knows, and probably knew before I did, that I couldn't leave you."

As they walked to Danny's Jeep Liberty, he explained about the money in the attaché case.

Kristen gasped, "Oh My God! This is bigger than just our little world."

"That's right. We've been let in on something that we can only speak of with each other. From what Albert said, I don't think anyone knows about this cash, or that he was even there as a driver. As far as the story goes, I can't say that I'm surprised. I teach about the Warren Commission, but I never believed that it got it right. And now we know. The proof was sitting in a back office of a restaurant in midtown New York City."

They reached the Liberty and then drove to Long Island to pick up Danny's luggage. The next stop was Kristen's apartment, where they would stay the night.

From her apartment, Danny made calls to his brothers who were "on the job." Without mentioning the cash, he gave them a condensed version of what took place at the club. Mario wanted to see him before Danny left, but was told there would be little time for a going away party. Mario understood.

After explaining it all to Tito, he asked Danny for a minute to think, and then Tito said, "I left one of my cell phones in the glove compartment. If you need to call, don't call anywhere but here at the precinct."

Danny nodded his head and then realized that he was on the phone and said, "Okay."

The call to his parent's house was unanswered, but Danny had already asked Tito to fill them in with a danger-free version.

Kristen's new bed was big enough for them, but not big enough to prevent a restless sleep. At 2 a.m., Kristen felt Danny's desire against her, and their mutual satisfaction was enough for them to sleep beyond the wake up time they had set at 5:30 a.m.

❧ CHAPTER TWENTY-FOUR ❧

They were on their way. The back seat of the Liberty was placed down to accommodate their luggage and the fuel was topped off. Armed with a road map of the entire United States, and Danny's knowledge of how to traverse Pennsylvania, their feeling of euphoria increased with each mile.

"Our first stop-over, I figure to be Columbus, Ohio. We're in no hurry, so there's no need to make this into a forced march; we'll get detailed maps as we go. Oh, and Tito said that he would call ahead to my cousin in New Mexico."

"I've never been out of the City, so my life is in your hands. And for that matter, just about everything else." She winked at Danny, who pretended not to have heard her, so she kicked him with her bare foot.

"Okay, okay I heard. I was just trying to make *you* the bad sexy one."

Kristen rode with her feet up on the dash board; her red shorts combined with a white blouse, tied at the waist, made Danny, for the moment, forget why they were on this trip.

"Nice cap," said Danny.

Kristen had on a white cap; her long blond pony tail trailed out of the opening in the back of the cap. She turned to acknowledge Danny's remark.

"What the hell is with that hat?" Danny questioned.

"What do you mean; I thought you just said that you liked it?" She not so innocently answered.

"The letter 'B' on the front, that's what the matter is!"

"The hat is white and matches my top and the 'B' is red and *it* matches my shorts, so what's the problem?"

"That's the problem; the 'B' is for Boston, like in, Red Sox? *We're* Yankee fans!"

"*We're* Yankee fans? I don't think so." Kristen's giggle was starting, complete with the tip of her tongue slipping out between her front teeth. Danny smiled back.

"Who would ever believe that I would be on vacation with a Red Sox fan?"

"Ditto." She answered and added, "What movie is that from?"

"Ghost." Danny answered and added. "Well okay, you being a sox fan will add to the action at the family Sunday dinners."

He looked at Kristen and had a strained expression on his face; she placed her hand on his.

"I guess I should've said when we clear this mess up, and when we return, it will be something to look forward to." Danny's voice was lowered.

They drove for a while in silence, with the only movement in the car coming when Kristen would, involuntarily, release tension by squeezing her toes together, causing Danny's attention to break from the road.

As they traveled on Interstate 80 through Pennsylvania,

Kristen noted. "I love how these tunnels are cut through the mountains."

Kristen's observation made Danny realize that he was not pointing out scenic events. "By the way, I forgot to mention that we passed the Delaware Water Gap a while back."

"You're fired!" Kristen brought her feet down off of the dash board to emphasize her point. "If you're going to point out points of interest one hundred miles *after* we pass them, then I'm the new vacation guide. Give me the maps, give me the books – you're through."

"I accept the firing like the man I am. Are you getting hungry?"

"Yes and I have to use the bathroom; us girls don't come with twenty gallon kidneys like you boys."

They pulled off at the next rest stop and stepped out into the heat. After cheese burgers and coffee at a fast food restaurant, they changed drivers.

"This doesn't mean that you become the guide, you're now the back-up driver."

Danny feigned dejection by lowering his head.

The pace had picked up.

"How does a small girl like you have such a heavy foot?"

"I don't know, do I? That's one of the benefits of not knowing your ancestry. I don't know about the winners and I don't have any losers to angst about. My history begins with me."

"And me with you." Danny said.

"Is that a commitment?" Kristen answered.

"Not at seventy miles an hour it isn't."

Kristen began to slow down and immediately pulled off of Interstate 80, and stopped in the breakdown lane.

"Well?" She said. "Is this slow enough?"

Danny was too surprised to do anything but smile. But, then he raised his finger, as if he had a trump card, and reached into the pocket of his jeans.

"I know this is a little sudden," he said.

Kristen's eyes grew wide.

"This is a token of my love."

He produced what looked to be a five carat diamond ring.

"It's adjustable," he noted.

Kristen bypassed the giggle and went right into a hearty laugh, much bigger then would be assumed for her size.

"Drive hard, laugh hard," said Danny.

"I love you too," Kristen answered as she pulled back onto the highway; still looking at the ring on her finger, "When did you have the time to order such a gem? No pun intended."

"At the last stop there was a vending machine for well heeled people, especially those with a dollar in quarters."

It was 6:30 p.m. when they arrived in Columbus, Ohio, and at the entrance of a Comfort Suites Hotel. Before checking to see if there were any rooms available, Danny put Tito's EZ Pass into its protective pouch, and into the glove compartment; there had not been any need for it for a while. Danny believed that it was a Northeast thing, and its use was over.

Kristen asked for a king size bed and was told that the total price was $84.02. Danny handed the desk clerk five crisp twenty dollar bills. The clerk took them and hesitated.

"They're new, but they're the old kind, without the color," said the clerk.

"You're right," said Danny. "They're new and old at the same time. My grandfather gave them to me for my birthday."

The clerk took one of the bills and went through a door behind the front desk. Almost immediately, he came back out and began processing their room. He gave them room keys for number 215 and explained where it was. Danny and Kristen went back out to the Liberty and unloaded their luggage.

They showered off their road sweat and changed clothes. Kristen put on jeans and a white tank top. Danny was almost matching with white short sleeved shirt.

"I'm not that hungry," said Kristen.

"Maybe because it's 7:30 and it's still in the 80's. What the hell is it going to be like as we head due west?" said Danny.

"Don't ask me, I'm just along for the ride."

"I like when you talk dirty," said Danny.

"Don't you ever think about anything else?"

"Sometimes, but this is not one of those times."

Nearby they found a fast food burger place that had air conditioning, and were surprised at how their appetite had returned.

"This bed has six pillows!" Kristen exclaimed.

"Just think. You can hit me six times without reloading."

They were the last words spoken before falling to sleep in each others arms, on one pillow.

❦ CHAPTER TWENTY-FIVE ❦

The door swung open, oak against mahogany trim, splintering the door stop and denting the floor molding. Six soldiers of the Stanuto Family stormed through and took their positions in the bar area. The advanced guard of the "Don" had preceded the arrival of "Big Carlo Stanuto." He was further flanked by two more bodyguards.

Albert was pre-warned by a call from the bartender and was out of his office – standing in front of Big Carlo. Words were not spoken, just a hand signal from the "Don," motioning a path to the back office.

Albert did not go behind, but stood in front of his desk. "Don Stanuto, what an honor." He said for the sake of Big Carlo's two men. Albert hesitated to kiss the Don's ring, a custom that was no longer being practiced.

"Yeah let's skip the fucking formalities. Last night I not only didn't get my fucking money, two of my men were treated like shit. I want you to tell me where I can find your bouncer?" Big Carlo turned and motioned to his bodyguards, who had followed him - lock step, to wait outside.

"I know his name and I know he has a girlfriend here. Is she working today?"

"She quit," Albert quickly responded.

With his men out of the office, and told to wait in the bar area, Big Carlo Stanuto's tone changed.

"You were my father's best friend. He chose you to be my godfather. I respect you. When you say you can't pay, I believe you. But, I have to play the game or else some *sfaccimme* (bastard) is going to smell blood and think I'm weak. This I can't have."

"They used strong arm tactics, Carlo. My man only came to my aid, he didn't start it."

"I figured that. Sam and Frankie are both hot heads; always looking to make a name for themselves. Tell this 'Danny' to stay away for a couple of weeks, by then all this will be done with. Something tells me that you've already told him."

Albert nodded, "I *did* tell him to stay away."

"The girl too?"

"I can't say definitely, but that's probably true. She called this morning and said that she had some family problems and needed some time off."

"Good, a couple of weeks should do it. In the meantime I'll smooth this over with my brother and have one of my personal 'associates' take over the collections."

"Thank you Carlo."

Big Carlo gestured his "your welcome" with a raised hand and then extended it for a handshake, signaling closure.

Albert waited for Big Carlo to leave before steadying himself with a hand on his desk.

🕉 CHAPTER TWENTY-SIX 🕉

Columbus, Ohio

In the morning they took advantage of the hotel's free breakfast. An employee, who, for years, had set up the cafeteria bar, was retiring, and a collection cup was made available. Danny put in a crisp twenty dollar bill.

As they made their choices and placed them on a tiny table, it wobbled, making their coffee spill. Danny folded a paper dish under one of the legs.

"See, I'm not without *other* skills!"

Kristen playfully struck him causing the table to wobble in spite of its stabilizer.

The Liberty was packed and by 10 a.m. they were on their way West on Interstate 70. At the Indiana state line they pulled into the welcome/rest area, had a soda, and picked up maps. Kristen grabbed some points of interest pamphlets.

"We may never come this way again and there might be something we would regret not seeing"

Danny agreed.

From this point, Kristen took over the driving toward Indianapolis, and Danny read her pamphlets.

"Well, for starters, we'll have to see the Indianapolis Speedway, let's see what else? Oh my God!"

"What Danny?"

"They have in Indianapolis, a tribute to every Congressional Medal of Honor winner for every war."

Kristen looked quizzically at Danny.

"My dad won that medal."

Kristen spoke without taking her eyes off of the road, "I don't know much about wars or medals, but that one I do know. It's the highest honor you can get. You must be so proud."

"I am."

There was silence as Kristen let Danny absorb what his father must have done to be awarded that medal.

"He never spoke about what he did to earn it. In fact I never even heard about it until they honored him at my Golden Gloves Championship Bout. It was obvious that he didn't want the publicity. But *I* would like to know what he did."

"Me too," said Kristen.

∾

At 12 noon they turned off of I-70 as Danny navigated them to West 16th Street and the Indianapolis Speedway. Kristen parked the Liberty in a field facing a large, impressive, building wall which read, "INDIANAPOLIS MOTOR SPEEDWAY – RACING CAPITAL OF THE WORLD" and over its front entrance, "HALL OF FAME."

A parking attendant approached.

"Could you please tell us how we get to go one lap around the speedway? Kristen asked.

"Yes, of course. You go into the museum and there's a booth in there where you can pick up your tickets."

"Thank you," she answered.

With their purchased tickets, they waited for the next tour bus. Once around entitled them to one small certificate each - "Completed one lap around Indianapolis '500' Mile Speedway." Wanting to get to the Memorial, they skipped the museum and pledged to do it on the way back home.

It was a short drive to the White River State Park and after crossing the small water-way, twice, by error, they came to the Congressional Medal of Honor Memorial.

There were twenty-seven curved glass walls etched with all of the names. A sign at the entrance said they become illuminated at dusk. Danny didn't know what year Hector won the medal, but there was an information locator. He put in "H-e-c-t-o-r L-o-p-e-z," as Kristen looked over his shoulder.

On the small screen appeared, *LOPEZ, HECTOR – Specialist Fourth Class, US Army, Company C, 2nd Battalion. Entered service at Fort Buchanan, Puerto Rico, Born 19 March 1947, San Juan, Puerto Rico. For conspicuous gallantry above and beyond the call of duty. 19 April 1968, Republic of Vietnam. When his unit came under heavy fire from the NVA, they retreated back to a safer position. With complete disregard for his own life, Specialist 4 Hector Lopez crawled over 100 feet without cover, to their former position, to aid three wounded members of his squad. This included squad leader, Lt. Charles Marchand, future United States Senator. He had just stabilized these men, when a NVA regular charged at him and was brought down by fire from his unit. It was during this time that he received three separate wounds. As this enemy soldier lay at his feet, Hector "Doc" Lopez ripped open the soldier's uniform and applied packing to his wound. Upon seeing this, the NVA ceased firing as did the US Forces. Many lives were saved this day due to the heroics and humanitarian act of Sp4 Hector Lopez.*

Danny's eyes were moist as were Kristen's.

Before leaving, they walked over to the glass panels covering Hector's service in Vietnam. The column read 1964-1973. Danny placed his hand on the glass etched with the name "Hector Lopez" and Kristen placed her hand on his.

It was 2 p.m. when they left Indianapolis and were on their way to Terre Haute, Indiana.

∞

They drove into the circular entrance to what looked like a new Holiday Inn. Rooms were available and Danny paid $116.68 and, again, the twenty dollar bills were called into question.

"They're old but new?" The desk clerk took off her glasses to get a closer look. And then, as was done in the last hotel, she took one of the bills and went through a door behind the counter. When she came out, she processed the payment without any further question.

"This inside courtyard or whatever you call it is so beautiful." Kristen exclaimed. "The water fall, the visible elevators, everything."

Their room was on the second tier which didn't require an elevator. A short stairway from the lobby and they were at their door.

"I see they have a laundry, and it's about *that* time," Kristen noted.

The hotel also had a restaurant, which was in the same direction as the laundry. Soap and softeners were purchased from a vending machine and their clothes were left washing while they had dinner. During the meal, Kristen made transfers from the washer to the dryer.

"I think in the morning, we should look for a bank and trade some of our 'old' money for new," said Danny. "Besides the new condition, I just happened to look at their date. They were printed in Dallas, Texas in 1963"

Kristen shivered.

Danny placed his hand on her shoulder. "It had the same effect on me."

After dinner they stopped by their room because Danny wanted to turn up the air conditioning. The after-dinner walk was cut short when they saw a strip mall across from the hotel; it was still almost 80 degrees. The only shop opened was a book store.

Danny bought two books on the "conspiracy theory" and Kristen chose a novel which was described on the back cover as, "a love story with murder and escape."

Kristen handed Danny her book.

Danny laughed. "Is this book about us?" He paid with the 1963 twenties with no questions asked.

"Each time we get change, I put it to our 'large purchase' supply, mainly, hotels. By now the room should be sufficiently cooled off."

"Why is it so important for the room to be cold, especially since you're Mr. Cool?"

"If I have to explain it, then I've cooled it off for nothing."

Kristen shook her head.

In the morning, Kristen noted a small brown line on her white shorts and the same mark on Danny's white tee shirt. As she looked further, it seemed to appear in some degree, on their other clothes.

A trip to the front desk had a visibly upset manager, asking if $50.00 would be enough of compensation. They agreed.

"We now have $50.00 of no problem money, but we need to do better than that," said Danny.

Kristen asked for the local yellow pages, from the very apologetic manager – more than anxious to please. They went to the closest three banks and at each of them, traded two hundred dollars of twenties for four fifties.

"I figure there would be fewer questions with small amounts." Danny said.

There were no questions.

Breakfast was served in the main dining area, while outside, rain began to fall. By the time they were ready to leave, the teeming rain had become windswept and gone sideways. The overhead closure of the main entrance provided little protection as they loaded their luggage. Afterwards, the gas stations overhead provided even less protection for Danny as he pumped. He paid with wet 1963 twenties.

∾

"I thought it couldn't rain any harder, I was wrong," said Kristen. "Why did I do my hair?" she added.

The St. Louis Gateway Arch appeared in the distance; its usual, gleaming stainless steel, dulled by the sweeping rain.

"Can't stop," said Danny.

"I know."

"Another one for the way back, I also wanted to see the Cathedral Basilica of St. Louis, since I read so much about it."

Kristen looked quizzical and Danny took note.

"When I was adopted, the Lopez family introduced me to religion. Up to that point I didn't have a god. I *hoped* for things in my life, but I didn't know how to pray, they taught me. I'm not a strict, follower of all the rules Catholic, but I *did* see the goodness of my adopting family. And that's what *I* adopted."

"Danny, I'm not patronizing you, but I don't know what I did to deserve you. How you handle life and how you treat me...." Kristen's voice trailed off.

"How about the way I treat life and how I handle you? Okay, okay, don't hit me. It's just that I don't take compliments easily. I apologize and I thank you. Now it's my turn. You had me at first touch. When I shook your hand over that bar, it was no longer *just* me"

They rode through the sheets of rain in silence. On both sides of the road, newly grown plants were floating on water covered fields.

"Those poor farmers," Kristen said. "How do you come back from all of this?"

"It's called resilience. I don't know how they do it, but they do."

The transition from I-70 to I-44 was made going through St. Louis.

"We'll stop over at Springfield, Missouri – maybe between 3 or 4 p.m."

Kristen nodded.

"You *can* say something – you're not just along for the *ride*," said Danny, smiling.

"No matter how I answer you, you're going to turn it around to mean something else, and we know what that something else is."

"And who was that last night, room service?" said Danny.

Kristen stared straight ahead, expressionless, as Danny drove.

∾

The rain did not let up during their drive to Springfield, Missouri. After an early dinner they read the books they had purchased in Terre Haute.

"It says here, and I've read this in other places," said Danny, "that Kennedy wanted to leave Vietnam, but that he, politically, couldn't do it until his second term. So instead of this war droning on, he could begin to get out in 1965. A lot of people would have lost a lot of money if that war ended. All of those *patriots*, and don't get me wrong, I love this country; my father won its highest medal. Of the 58,000 dead, how much less would that number have been? And *who are* these people that always need an enemy? Now we know why, that after the autopsy, his brains were lost. They might have contained fragments from a .44 caliber bullet, and *that* would be the end of the one man - one gun fairytale."

In the morning there was a complimentary breakfast.

"S O S, I love it!" Danny exclaimed.

"It says creamed beef, what's S O S?" Kristen asked.

"Well," Danny said in a low voice, "It's an old Army term that I learned from my father – 'Shit on the Shingle.' We had it once while on a family vacation - he only told us boys."

The rain was at its same intensity when they left for Oklahoma City. Kristen was driving.

"I can't travel the speed limit, it's too dangerous," said Kristen.

"The Liberty won't know who's driving," said Danny.

"Very funny, Danny."

The rain kept coming. The radio was reporting floods in the areas they just left; with parts of Indianapolis were under water. The rain had gone on for such a long time that the slight lessening was not noticed for several miles.

"Hey, it's stopping," said Danny.

As they drove through Tulsa, the weather change was abrupt. The sun shone through the disappearing clouds causing vapors to rise from the road. Because of the wet weather, Danny and Kristen had forgotten how hot this part of the country can get.

"Oh my god, bring back the rain," said Kristen.

Danny drove to another Holiday Inn and checked in. "Are we becoming creatures of habit?" asked Kristen.

They left to visit the Memorial.

"The chairs, the reflecting pool, all in honor of innocent

children caught up in a mad mans mind." Kristen said, as she shook her head.

They held hands as they observed a statue of Jesus with his back to the Memorial.

Their morning began with the temperature of 85 degrees. Danny started the days driving, taking I-40 out of Oklahoma toward Texas.

✄ CHAPTER TWENTY-SEVEN ✄

Dallas, Texas

Colonel Floyd Cooper waited at his four pillared front entrance for Aubrey Kincaid to arrive. Kincaid's Mercedes could be seen off in the distance, throwing up dust, as it wound its way toward the main house. It entered the circular driveway and stopped at the steps leading up to where Cooper was standing. Both Cooper and Kincaid were seventy-seven years old and both had Texan drawls.

"This better be important; you made me waste a Viagra pill," said Kincaid.

"Well before you get a hard-on for the wrong reasons, come in and hear me out." Cooper pointed him in the direction of the library.

Carved and inlaid wood shelves held the books in place – right to the ceiling. His wife had read them all. When she died, his succession of flighty 50 year olds, were not around for their intellect.

"Join me in a bourbon Aubrey?"

"Okay, but this better be good."

"Then I guess I'll get right to the point. Ten twenty dollar bills surfaced the other day on ebay. The serial numbers were in sequential order."

"What the fuck is that supposed to mean? And what the hell is ebay?"

"Ebay is electronic classified ads. The currency was dated 1963 and minted in Dallas; they were from a special batch, a *very* special batch," he repeated.

"What the hell....?"

"You know what this means?" said Cooper.

Cooper answered his own question. "It means that someone might have the knowledge and proof, AND PROOF," he repeated, "of what really happened that day. And I don't have to tell you that when the light of day shines on how our money was made, the killings that were done to make it, and most of all, the existence of a second government, it'll be more than shit hitting the fan, it'll be a fucking rain of diarrhea. Our ability to make money by always needing an enemy, our organization, our CIA connections, and our extremist division would be on review for all to see. It would be like a nuclear explosion."

"What can we do?" asked Kincaid, with a catch in his throat.

"I've already notified Shultz and his 'Americans for God' idiots. And *our* Agents are working on tracing and tracking the individual or individuals passing this money. All of the *guinea*s connected to this money are dead and until now, nobody really thought about this cash; it was assumed to be spent. The fact, that after all this time, it's turning up, makes this a serious matter. You and I, we're old horses. The barn has plenty of young colts, most of whom only surmise what might have come down that day. There are only a few of us left and it is up to us to preserve the way history was written."

The phone rang.

"Cooper here! Yes, I understand. Get an Agent over there. There's got to be surveillance tapes, if not a description from the teller. Remember it's *government* business. If they're not local, then check all of the hotels in the area. Y'all get on it and get back to me pronto!"

He turned to Kincaid, "It seems that a teller exchanged his own money for the twenties, because he thought they might be worth something - lucky for us he placed them on ebay, which gives contact information."

They finished their bourbon as a second one was brought to them.

CHAPTER TWENTY-EIGHT

The Liberty's outside temperature gauge registered 101 degrees, and its air conditioning was set at the highest level. Kristen had her bare feet up on the dash, and was dressed for the extreme temperature in a khaki mini skirt and white halter top.

Danny noticed her toes squeezing and un-squeezing at a rapid pace; more than usual.

"Is there something wrong?" he asked.

"Well yes, I need to use the bathroom. You reminded me, that with these temperatures, I need to stay hydrated by drinking a lot; well this is what happens. And don't say that I should have taking care of this at the hotel. There wasn't a need then. But right now there is a *big* need." Kristen raised her eyebrows and cocked her head for Danny's response.

"Okay, okay, there was a sign about five miles ago that advertised a truck stop in ten miles. We'll be there soon."

Her continued rapid toe movement caused Danny to go over the speed limit.

"There's another sign," Danny pointed out. "We'll be there in two miles – less than two minutes."

The truck stop was on the other side of I-40. Danny took the off-exit, went under the overpass, and pulled into the parking area. Kristen jumped out.

"I'm going to check out the fast food and see what maps they have," he said to Kristen's fleeing body. "I'll meet you back here," he added, but Kristen was already out of range.

Danny decided to use the men's room, and before heading back to the parking lot, he scanned the restaurant's menu and then checked out the gift shop for maps.

Kristen wasn't back yet. Danny lowered all of the windows and put back the driver's seat. For the first time he noticed the activity in the parking lot. *Man, there are a lot of motorcycles here – must be a cruise or something.* He then looked closer and couldn't believe his eyes as they focused in on all of the leather jackets and the behavior of people who were wearing them. The top rocker (emblem) said, "VULTURES."

"Kristen, where's Kristen!" he said out loud.

Danny raised the windows, jumped out of the Liberty and ran toward the truck stop diner. He stopped at the men's room and looked for, and found a sign with an arrow, which read "ladies." He followed the arrow around a corner and came upon a large man leaning against a wall with his left arm. From between his legs he could see Kristen's fancy green sandals. He then heard her say. "Don't you fucking touch me!"

"Hey man, what's going on?" asked Danny.

The *apartment building,* turned his head to the right, but because of his thick neck, his upper torso also turned. Danny could now see a leather jacket draped over a railing. Kristen was still blocked by the huge torso.

"Get the fuck outta here before I eat your motherfucking face." His lips hardly moved.

Danny took in the entire picture. "Scud," the name on the jacket tag, was taller, and had him out-weighed by more than a hundred pounds. There would not be any negotiation.

Danny stepped to his left and hit Scud in his left kidney; first punch, albeit illegal, since the Golden Gloves. He hit him again and again and again as if his kidney was a focus mitt. It was too fast and too painful for Scud to launch any offensive. He was on his knees when Danny bent down and hit him two more times in the same kidney. He went face down making growling and gurgling sounds. Danny reached over Scud's seething mass and plucked Kristen into his arms. He began running to the exit. "We've got to get away from here."

"Danny! Danny!"

"What?"

"You're still carrying me!"

"Oh, sorry." He put her down, and now they *both* ran toward the exit.

"The bottom rocker, that's that back patch, said 'Ohio.' It'll be good it they're going that way, opposite from us. So what happened back there?"

"He must have seen me go in and was waiting for me when I came out. Funny, I wasn't nervous, I just knew you would come for me."

Danny opened the passenger door and ran around to the driver's side. They weaved their way through a lot full of motorcycles and leather jackets, went under the over pass and onto I-40 heading West. Danny drove with his eye on the rear view mirror. He saw a road side sign advertising food and gas in twenty miles.

"That's a long way."

"What's a long way," asked Kristen.

"Sorry, I was just thinking out loud, that's our next chance to get off, if we have to."

Danny had the Liberty up to eighty miles per hour – while still watching what was behind them.

Kristen heard it first, "Is that a helicopter?"

"Those are bikes." Danny answered.

"Bikes?"

"Yes Bikes, like in motorcycles." Danny shook his head.

It was a faint, low humming sound, growing in its intensity.

"My God, Danny! They have guns. I saw one in that Scud guys belt."

Danny had diverted his attention from the rear view mirror to the trough or ditch which separated East and West traffic of I-40.

"I can see them! I can see them! They look like a shimmering mirage. That noise is really getting to me." Kristen's voice was shaking.

Danny changed to the left lane and began to slow down.

"What are you doing?" she gasped.

"I'm slowing down."

"I can see that. Why? Why?"

"Now don't panic. Be that same brave person who was dealing with Scud ball back there."

"Danny, they're almost here! And I *am* panicking."

At twenty miles per hour, he turned the Liberty down toward the ditch. The rain had filled the trough, which Danny thought to be about fifteen feet wide with a couple of inches of rain covered mud. As he got to the edge of the ditch he stopped the Liberty and put it into four wheel drive - low. They started across at a snails pace.

"Can't we go any faster?" asked Kristen. "Jesus, Danny, they're here!"

The motorcycles arrived at the top of the highway as the Liberty slowly drew itself through the muck and now had its front wheels on dry land. Danny stopped and put the transmission into regular four wheel drive; he gunned it upward toward the east bound traffic. At the highway he took it out of four wheel drive and merged into the fast lane; in no time they were up to eighty miles per hour.

"They can't follow us, because they can't cross that muck. And they can't jump over it while heading *down*. We're safe for now. We'll go two exits and then head back going west."

After two exits they did as Danny had planned and reversed their direction back the other way.

"You were pretty brave back there at the truck stop," said Danny.

"Like I said, I just knew you would come. But let me ask you this, how do *you* stay so cool?"

"Well we both can't be saying, 'Oh shit we're all going to die!'"

"I wouldn't say that, because I don't talk like that."

"Now wait a minute, I heard what you called 'Scud man'

back there or is that manner of talk only reserved for danger and sex?"

Kristen's smile, complete with tongue between her teeth, was her answer.

As they went past the point on the highway where they had crossed to the east side, they saw the torn turf where the motorcycles went down and the Liberty's tracks went up. They both looked, but said nothing.

At the Texas border there was a Visitor's Welcome Center where Danny got some maps and Kristen picked up some special interest pamphlets; plus "Don't Mess With Texas" car stickers. After using the facilities, they went over to the complimentary coffee sign. While Kristen was making their cups, two Texas highway patrolmen came into the Center and over to the coffee urn.

Danny asked them, "How do you stay so cool and neat in this weather?"

"We drive cool cars," one of them said. He pointed to a Mustang in the parking lot.

"It's his," the other one said. He gets the unmarked cool one and I get to drive the decorated one."

"That's not cool, man, that's a hot car."

The troopers laughed and one of them said, "Y'all have a good one."

As they walked away one of them said to the other, "New Yorkers! You can always tell New Yorkers."

❧ CHAPTER TWENTY-NINE ❧

Terre Haute, Indiana

The bank was not busy. Three tellers were on duty, but only one had a customer; no one was waiting in the platform area. Mark Tolson went directly to one of the platform managers; each one had a glass enclosed office. A bespectacled middle aged woman was looking down, as he entered.

She glanced up over her eyeglasses, "Can I help you?"

"Yes ma'am, I'm looking for the bank manager."

"I'm Mrs. Finch, the assistant manager, the manager, Mrs. Kraft, is not here today." She held out her hand.

"Well then, maybe you can help me. I'm Agent Tolson with the CIA." He showed her his ID and took her hand.

"I'll do my best, Agent Tolson."

"One of our agents passed away very suddenly, yesterday, and we're trying to locate his son, who is on vacation in this area. Are all of your tellers here today?"

"Yes, we're a small bank and only hire what we need. We don't have any part-timers and no one, at this time, is on vacation."

"I see that you have two female tellers and one male. May I start with male teller?"

"Yes, you can use this office." Mrs. Finch stepped out and called the teller in.

The teller needed a haircut; his white shirt was open to the second button and his tie was pulled down from his neck.

"I'm Agent Tolson with the CIA and you are?"

"Brian Peters." He answered as he swallowed.

They shook hands.

Tolson looked down at his small notebook, it read, "Brian Peters."

"I'll get right to the point; you placed for sale on eBay, ten, twenty dollar bills. I'd like to know how you came about getting them?"

"I…I replaced them from a deposit I got. Am I going to get in trouble? People do that here all of the time with coins. I know it's probably wrong…I made sixty dollars…I'll give it back to the bank." His hands shook as he buttoned his shirt and pulled up his tie. He wiped his sweaty brow with his shirt sleeve.

"Calm down. I don't give a fuck what you did with the bills, what I want to know is if you could identify the person you got them from. Can you remember what the time frame was from when you made the *transaction*, to when you put them on eBay?"

"I…I'm not sure. Maybe one day, m..maybe two days, I'm not sure."

Peters slumped back in his chair as Tolson called Mrs. Finch back into the office.

"Do you have a service that takes care of the surveillance tapes?"

"No we don't, like I said we're a small bank, so our tapes are kept in the basement."

"Good I need to see the tapes for a three day period."

Peters was on unsteady legs as both he and Tolson followed Mrs. Finch to the basement.

"That's him! That's him!" Peters shouted.

Tolson downloaded the picture to his laptop, thanked Mrs. Finch and waved off shaking Peters' sweaty hand. Before leaving the bank's air conditioning, he opened his local map and saw that the closest hotel was the Holiday Inn.

Tolson identified himself, showed his credentials and told the same sad story. No one on the current shift could identify the picture, so he booked a room and left a printed copy at the front desk.

"As soon as he can be recognized, please call me at once. I don't care what the time is."

Tolson went up to his room, thankful for a small break. Maybe I'll even get breakfast in the morning. Two hours later the phone rang.

"Mr. Tolson? This is the front desk. The reservation clerk, who took care of the person you are interested in, has come on duty."

"I'll be right down."

Tolson was introduced, "This is Ms. Weston."

Her face was flawless, her smooth brown skin was radiant and her smile was captivating. The dull uniform could not hide the body of a model. Tolson for a moment forgot that he was an *Apostle.*

"I understand that you can identify this individual?" He held up his copy; while she looked down at a picture that was given to her.

"Yes I certainly can. I remember that they gave me brand new, old twenty dollar bills to pay for their room."

"They?" asked Tolson.

"Yes, they were a couple, but I didn't see any rings, so I'm assuming that she was his girl friend."

"First of all *you* don't assume anything, that's my job, Ms. Weston"

Teri Weston was taken aback by Tolson's manner.

"I didn't mean to step on your toes, so to speak, I just thought you could use that information."

She opened a computer screen.

"His name is Danny Lopez." She purposely didn't elaborate.

Tolson looked over her shoulder and took down the rest of the information, but not without looking down her white blouse.

Bastard, she thought.

Before driving back to the airport, he made a call to Washington, D.C.

"His name is Danny Lopez, 745 Orchard Street, Oyster Bay, New York. We're on it and it won't be long now."

❧ CHAPTER THIRTY ❧

New York City

The telephone rang; a soft ring.

"You know who this is?"

"Yes."

"We might have a very old problem?"

"So long ago."

"Yes it has been, but there might have been a serious oversight."

"I see. What do you propose to do?"

"We need to talk. Meet me at 'Lucky's' on 8th and 44th tomorrow at 8 a.m."

"Okay."

The old man entered "Lucky's" Diner and slowly limped to a booth in the back. He sat facing the door. Moments later a second elderly man arrived. The "old man" raised his hand to get his attention. The second man's gate was strong and his frame was sturdy.

"Its been a long time. You look good." He said to the "old man."

"Nice of you to say. It is you who has stayed younger and fit." He answered with a German accent.

Victor Strom *had* stayed fit, while Fredrick Shultz had tried to stay one step ahead of the FBI for war crimes they believed he had committed.

Shultz spoke again. "When we took out the *guineas*, as the *Apostles* wanted, I thought our job was over. But it seems that *they*, not us, in their haste to finish them off, missed an important bit player. Joey Pinto didn't drive himself from New York to New Orleans, he had a driver. And he must have given him some of the money we gave him. Outside of the 'Apostles' and us, he might be the only one in the country that knows the Warren Report is a piece of *scheisse* (shit). You understand, that except for us, and unlike the 'Apostles,' our branch of this organization does not know about its role back in 1963. The *Apostles* have stayed young, with its members of congress, court appointments and high placed business executives. We've just gotten older."

"What are we to do?" Strom asked.

"We sit tight until we hear from the *Apostles*, and they tell us who we have to take out. Our new recruits are coming from the U.S. Military, of all places, where they learn high-tech killing; except they're meaner and more ruthless than we ever were. Some choose to run around the Southwest and play insurgents and others like Erik Posser, assimilate into normal lives. He's as tough as they come, and as soon as we know where to send him, he will do what is necessary to fix this problem. Of course, he doesn't know *what* he is fixing. As far as he's concerned, he's doing it for God and Country."

"The *Apostles* still need us to do their dirty work. The

greaseballs were as big a set-up as Oswald was. They took care of our problem and then we took care of them – one by one, making it look like a mob war."

"Let's not give them all the credit. Are you not forgetting my role?" said Strom.

"No I'm not, but you were using a good German rifle, a Mauser, not that piece of *scheisse* Italian rifle."

They finished their coffee and went out into the warm air.

❦ CHAPTER THIRTY-ONE ❦

At mid afternoon, Danny and Kristen arrived in Amarillo, Texas. Their choice of hotels remained the same – get the free buffet breakfast that Kristen likes and she wanted Danny to get his S O S. The hotel was right across from a large steak house.

"If we're in Texas we have to eat steak!" said Danny.

"That sounds good, but at this point I'll take any restaurant, food chain or whatever, as long as it has air conditioning. I don't understand the dry heat theory. It's humid and its been over hundred degrees for days. If I wore anything less, I'd be arrested."

The steak house across from the parking lot was not the one Danny had read about in the pamphlet.

"That's not the one in the pamphlet. But it does look nice; we can go to this one…."

"I know," Kristen interrupted, "On the way back."

After settling into their room, they found the pamphlet, and then went out and found the steakhouse.

The young hostess sat them down next to a platform, which had on it, a table and a time clock. If a customer could eat a 72 ounce steak with all of the trimmings, in one hour, they wouldn't have to pay. No one, this evening, was taking up the challenge.

"Gino!" They both said together.

"He would certainly be able to beat the clock," said Danny.

Kristen agreed and for a moment they thought about their life as it used to be.

"All this will soon be over, and then we can go back home. In fact I've been meaning to give Tito a call"

He used Kristen's cell phone to call the precinct. Danny was told that Tito was away from his desk, but that he would be 'returning shortly.'

Wandering musicians came by and Danny gave them a twenty dollar bill to play "On the Road Again."

As dessert was served, Kristen's phone rang.

"Tito? Man it's good to hear your voice."

"Danny, I was going to call you. I have some sad news. Last night there was a robbery at Alberto's and both Albert and someone named Gino Balletta, were shot to death. Was that his son?"

"I can't believe it! I can't believe it!" Danny repeated, and then answered Tito's question. "No, Gino was his nephew."

"What, Danny?" Kristen asked, as she grabbed Danny's arm.

"Albert and Gino were both killed last night during a robbery."

"Oh my God! Oh my God!" Kristen put her hands to her face.

"I just told Kristen. How could this happen – they were *protected*. Do you know what I mean? They had mob protection. He brought that protection by buying linen. This shouldn't be happening, Bro. I mean they were protected. I know that I keep repeating myself, but that doesn't happen to people like that."

"Danny, there's something else, and I don't know what it means, but Senator Marchand, Dad's friend, was working with another senator on some piece of legislature, and noticed your name scribbled on a pad on his desk. He was smart enough not to call it to the senator's attention. He first thought that it might have something to do with boxing because it had boxer written next to your name, but then he thought otherwise. He didn't like it, and is going to look into it. The good news, if there's any, is that this senator doesn't know that Senator Marchand is connected to us."

"I don't like it either," said Danny

"This senator is always spouting out biblical terms and according to Marchand, if he could, he would wear the flag on his forehead. That's all well and good, but he believes that America is being taken over by some foreign power. Dad always says that when a person is overly adamant about some evil, they sometimes are that very evil. When you get to our cousins, call me and maybe by then I'll have some better news. Later Bro."

"Stay safe Tito." Danny closed the cover on the cell phone.

"I know these things happen, but this is too close," said Danny. "I don't know about you, but I just lost my appetite for this desert," he added.

"Me too," said Kristen.

"This is the last night that we'll spend on the road, before we get to my cousins," said Danny as they lay side by side on their large hotel bed.

Kristen slid closer and into Danny's arms.

"I feel safe now."

❧ CHAPTER THIRTY-TWO ❧

Washington, D.C./Dallas, Texas

"Hello Cooper?"

"This *is* Cooper. Speak up, hearings not what it used to be."

"You don't remember this voice? You old fart!"

"Parsons! How the hell are you? I was wondering who had this number; it hasn't rung in a long time."

"Unfortunately, with our *problem*, we may be communicating more often, but hopefully not. I have some information that you can pass on to Shultz. The subject's name is Danny Lopez. Lucky for us, he worked a week in June and showed up on a New York State quarterly payroll report. He was employed at, get this, a restaurant that was a former strip club. It just so happens that the owner can be traced back to Joey Pinto; remember him?"

"Jesus Christ!" gasped Cooper.

"It seems that the owner, Albert Balletta, drove Pinto to the *job site*. We had assumed that Pinto had driven himself. He must have given Balletta some of his money. We don't know this for sure, but it's a pretty good bet that this is the way it went down. Here is what we do know, for sure. He's traveling with a girl; that he's a Golden Gloves champion boxer; that he has twenty dollar bills which we thought were long gone, and his ride is a black Jeep Liberty. And what we don't know, and need to find out about, is the girl – does she come from a privileged family or even one that has ties to the *Apostles*. That could be a problem. Another thing we don't know is what direction they're going. We're assuming the worst – that he knows what the money was for."

"Where did y'all last trace him to?"

"Terre Haute, Indiana. He may be heading further West, or he might be going north. This is *Apostle* business – I don't want local law enforcement or the FBI to get wind of this; we've never been able to crack *that* fucking group. We got Judges, Senators, House Members, CIA agents up the wazoo, but as far as the FBI is concerned, nada."

"Y'all sound confident," said Cooper

"I am. We'll get him, the girl, and anybody else that gets in our way of running things. Albert Balletta has already been taken care of. But we need Shultz to take care of this Lopez problem. This is what he does best."

"I'll call Shultz right now."

"Good, let me know how it goes. Remember to call me on my secure line, and I will do likewise at your number."

Senator Conrad Parsons closed the phone and looked, again, at the small piece of paper with "Danny Lopez" written on it. "Fucking *spic* bastard!" he said too loud.

From outside his close door, came a woman's voice, "Did you want me Senator Parsons?"

"No everything's just fine, just fine," he grimaced.

❧ Chapter Thirty-Three ❧

Dallas, Texas/New York City

Fifteen minutes after detailing the information about Danny, Cooper made another call to the same number.

"Hello Schultz? Cooper, again. I'm reading from an article in our local newspaper that's very interesting. It says that a 'Vulture,' that's a motorcycle gang member, was punched into a coma and hospitalized. Now I understand from the paper that this 'Vulture' member is some bad hombre. A quote from one of his fellow gang members went something like this, 'you could hit him over the head with a two by four and he wouldn't feel it.' The paper said 'punched.' Our boy is a boxer, is he not? And get this; they chased him and a girl in a small, black, SUV. Sounds like the Jeep Liberty ID we got from the hotel registration. Get a man on this immediately. They're heading west to New Mexico on I-40"

"I will."

Cooper did not give any further response and the telephone connection was terminated.

A night flight on a private jet originating from Indiana, with a final destination to Amarillo, Texas, was booked in the name of Erik Posser; waiting for him in Texas would be a special car and a large black bag.

❦ CHAPTER THIRTY-FOUR ❦

The free breakfast, S O S and all, lacked that spark as in the past. Most of the conversation revolved around packing the Liberty, and Danny being the first to drive.

"I've never seen speed limits like these, and *still* I'm being passed," said Danny. He mentioned the vast wind farm units off in the distance and then drew silent.

Kristen's feet were not up on the dash as usual, but placed on the seat; her arms wrapped around her knees in an almost fetal position. She nodded and gave forced smiles, in response to Danny's remarks.

"I'm worried, Danny. I'm *very* worried. It's no longer a mob thing. This is something else, something very sinister, and I feel that we may never be able to go back to the lives we had."

"I feel the same way, but I'm trying not to think about it. Albert and Gino being killed, and my name scribbled on some senator's pad? It's all connected in some way, but how? Albert told me that after he, somehow, was overlooked, one by one, all of the major and minor players involved in the assassination were systematically eliminated; especially the Italians and he knows it wasn't a mob war. So who? And maybe they're still around."

After another car passed them and was long gone, there was not a car to be seen in the front or in the rear. The monotony caused by the lack of scenery was hypnotic and dangerous at over 70 miles per hour. The hypnosis was broken as they past two roadside signs within feet of each other. One of them advertised a "Religious Revival Center" the other told of the "Largest Triple XXX Center," both at the next exit. Kristen's giggle caused Danny to say, "Thank you."

Danny saw the flashing lights through his rear view mirror. They were off in the distance, but closing fast. He was driving in the right hand lane and had been letting "the rest of the world" as he stated it, pass him by. Even though he was not exceeding the speed limit, he slowed to just under 70 MPH. He did this as a courtesy, so the official vehicle, or what ever it was, could pass him safely. It didn't.

"What the hell? He's practically in our trunk, if we had one!"

It was Danny's first mention of the approaching vehicle.

"What, what's going on?" asked Kristen.

Danny slowed down, and the edging even closer of the flashing lights, made him pull off of the road.

He turned to Kristen. "I hope this has nothing to do with that motorcycle business."

The unmarked Impala, with its magnetic bubble light, instead of stopping behind them, swerved in front of the Liberty and stopped at an angle.

"That's unusual," he said. "Why would he block us? And where was his siren?"

The officer in full highway patrol uniform including a straw cowboy hat, stood at the Liberty's driver side door.

"Let me see your license."

Danny showed him his New York license. It was quickly given back to him.

"Step out of the vehicle."

As the officer was stepping backwards, Danny, using both of his hands, swung his door open, knocking the trooper to the ground.

"DANNY WHAT ARE YOU DOING!" Kristen screamed and placed her hands along side of her face.

Danny was out of the Liberty as the trooper was picking himself up. The trooper was on his feet a lot faster than Danny figured. But because he drew his gun rather than attack, the moment gave Danny a chance to come over his right hand pistol draw with a punch. It missed the trooper's head and landed on his shoulder. The trooper managed to hold on to his weapon and was bringing it level, again, when Danny grabbed his arm and lifted the trooper's gun hand, high over his head. With his left leg, the trooper kicked Danny in the right hip causing Danny to fall forward, still holding the trooper's gun hand in the air. Danny's momentum carried him forward and the trooper backwards; his head hitting the top of the, still open door of the Liberty.

Kristen was at Danny's side.

"What are you doing, he's a police officer for god's sakes! Have you gone mad?"

"No, but this is not a police officer, either. He didn't do the ten point check. He only asked me for my driver's license;

it was obvious that my name is all he wanted. He didn't have a Texan drawl or a name tag, and he has an expensive 45 caliber gun with a rosewood handle, instead of Sig 226, 9 mm, like those troopers had at the Welcome Center. And lastly, this sticker here, says that it's a rental car; not a high powered vehicle at all. Our Jeep Liberty could give it a run for its money. Well maybe not outrun, but stay even – after I cross over to the other side of the highway."

"How could you joke at a time like this?"

"When I'm nervous I try for humor. And I *am* a little nervous." Danny looked down on the man lying on his stomach. "Well look at this, more proof that we have a fake cop."

"This is definitely not the usual back-up gun."

Danny took the weapon from the man's back holster and held it up, "This, Kristen, is a genuine German Luger. It says here 1941 and he scratched a Nazi swastika into the metal. What the hell does that mean?" Danny put it into his pocket. Looking down at the unconscious man, he saw the outline of a wallet in his back pocket and pulled it out. "It says here his name is Erik Posser. He has an Indiana driver's license, a couple of credit cards and an ID card from something called, 'American's for God.' I don't like it." When he put the wallet back into Posser's pocket, he noticed a cell phone lying on the ground, and handed it to Kristen.

Danny started the Impala's engine, drove it to the edge of the breakdown area, slightly set the parking break, and put the transmission into "park."

"What are you going to do?" asked Kristen.

Danny didn't respond to Kristen's question, but said, "Please give me a hand with *Lugar Man*."

As they dragged Posser to the open door of the Impala, Danny took the Luger out of his pocket and put in on top of the accelerator. The motor was still running.

"Hurry I see some cars coming."

They lifted Posser and threw him across the accelerator making the engine rev higher; his legs were sticking out of the open door.

"Step back!" he said to Kristen as he reached over Posser, and put the Impala in drive; keeping the parking break engaged. The Impala strained against its break and slowly went down a steep slope - Danny jumped backwards. The car settled into thick brush, just missing a cement drainage tunnel. Cars were whizzing by as Danny and Kristen got back into the Liberty.

"We can't go to my cousins and bring this pestilence down on them. I'm calling Tito and then we're getting lost."

Kristen nodded her head.

❦ CHAPTER THIRTY-FIVE ❦

Dallas, Texas/Washington, D.C.

"He what?"

"Shultz says he's lost contact with him. Last thing he heard from his man 'Posser,' was that 'he has them in his sights.' Now he's not answering his cell phone," said Cooper.

"What do we know about this 'Posser?'" asked Parsons.

"I asked Schultz that same question. Posser is military trained-Special Forces; well schooled in martial arts. He's supposed to be the real deal, without a conscience."

"Yeah well I don't know how it looks to you, but it seems that Danny boy got the best of him, and before that, he put a Herculean motorcycle gang member in the hospital; which makes 'Lopez' the super hero, not this guy Posser. We've obviously underestimated him. I didn't want to open ourselves up to any scrutiny, but I'm going to put some of *our* agents in the area and see what they can come up with."

"That's a good idea; meanwhile, I'll keep you informed as to Posser."

∾

Phone Call – Two hours later

"I heard from Schultz. The Texas Highway Patrol found Posser, dazed, and climbing up an embankment; his car lying in thick brush. They arrested him for impersonating a police officer."

"Shit," said Parsons.

"Don't worry I've already straightened it out, and he's back on the job. All charges were dismissed; got him recognized as a CIA 'associate,' thanks to our 'Apostles.' There wasn't any problem with gun permits, since Texas recognizes Indiana licenses. We're back on track."

"We still don't have Lopez," noted Parsons.

"We'll get 'em. They're in *my* part of the country now"

"I hope you're right. And that being in *your* part of the country isn't the same as 'I have them in my sights.'"

✖ CHAPTER THIRTY-SIX ✖

"It'll be another hour before we cross into New Mexico. They call this the Panhandle Plains, and it sure lives up to its name. And *this* is some of what they gave to the American Indian - hardscrabble land. Forget a rake; you'd need a jack hammer to plant seed."

Kristen was back in her fetal position. "I wonder what kind of progress we've *really* made since it was the Wild West. How free are we? That guy you threw off the side of the road had it in his mind to kill you, and probably me too."

"I don't want to scare you, but you're right. He wasn't going to arrest us; he couldn't, he wasn't a real cop. I think we both know what we've uncovered. The group, the people, maybe even a society that existed in 1963 is alive today. I'm sorry I dragged you into all of this."

"If you remember, I asked to be dragged."

"But not into this mess," Danny quickly countered.

"I don't care and I won't be a burden – you'll see."

Danny took Kristen's hand.

∾

They crossed over into New Mexico.

"Even though we're not going to go to your cousins, somehow I feel safer in New Mexico."

"Don't let 'Luger Man' taint your feelings toward Texas. Remember, he wasn't from Texas."

"You're right and they *do* have good steaks. So now what's the plan?" asked Kristen.

"Glad you asked. My plan, which is more of an idea, is to get deeper into this State, get off the main roads, and find a place where we can hide. We need to get this car out of circulation. 'Luger Man' knew us by our car."

Before reaching Albuquerque, Danny turned off of I-40 onto uncharted roads.

"Do you have any input, because at this point I could use something better than trying to get lost? Hey look at that sign!" Danny was pointing to a metal sign.

He slowed to get a better look. The "Do Not Pass" sign had been shot at so many times that the "Do Not" was almost obliterated.

"Danny, I've been meaning to ask you, how do you know so much about guns?"

"It's all Tito's fault, and his being a cop. All boys want to become a policeman, at one time, and some do. He convinced *me*, but not Mario, that, by having a gun, wasn't just an NRA thing. He said that it's too late for us to become like Europe; that the Second Amendment, in theory and in practice, sets us apart as Americans. Mario deplores guns, likewise, my father who saw enough, and the girls are split. My mother is a nay and my sister Maria doesn't think it's a bad idea. So there you have the whole Lopez gun story."

They drove on.....over narrow winding roads.

❦ CHAPTER THIRTY-SEVEN ❦

Washington, D.C.

Richard Steinitz was as fit at sixty-one as he was at twenty-four. His mind was quick and he was able to keep buried, the horrific memories it held. But a phone call from an old friend caused that memory to come barreling to the top. He waited outside of the senate office of former New York State Senator and now United States Senator, Lt. Charles Marchand.

"You can go in now," said Ms. Ramirez, who had moved with Marchand to the federal government.

"Been a long time, Duke," preceded an embrace of two former warriors.

"I never lost track of you Dick, just never could put the time aside – my fault."

"Nobody's fault, a telephone rings both ways. Anyway we're here now, for whatever the reason."

"Like I said, you may have been lost in my physical world not in spirit. I know you had a exemplary career with the FBI, and have a successful private investigation company."

"You haven't done too shabby, either. You did something unheard of by taking the City vote and being elected the first

Republican Senator from New York in over twenty years," said Steinitz.

"It was a very humbling event by having many Democrats vote for me. But as you know, neither of us would have ever been, if it wasn't for the actions of Hector Lopez. And now he needs our help."

"I will do anything, Duke, anything at all for that man." Tears glistened in his eyes as he remembered lying next to Marchand, while a young medic worked over them.

"It's Hector's son, Danny, who needs our help. He's stumbled upon something very big, very dangerous, and I'm afraid, very sinister. I'm in contact with his brother Tito, who's a New York City cop, and he tells me that Danny was run off the road by an imposter Texas cop. He *was* in Texas, but I'm not sure where he is now."

"Danny Lopez, I remember a pretty good fighter in the New York Gloves or whatever it's called, Golden Gloves, but he was white."

"Danny is Hector's son. He adopted him out of an abusive foster care home."

"He doesn't stop, does he? That big heart of his knows no bounds," said Steinitz.

"What I need from you is to find out what you can about a Senator Conrad Parsons. I want to know who he calls, who he eats with, lays with, and what connection he might have to an Erik Posser. He's that imposter cop from Texas. Danny had the smarts to confiscate Posser's cell phone. It didn't have any names attached to the in-coming or out-going numbers, but Danny *did* read them off to his brother Tito. Tito called Hector and Hector called me. Here are those numbers."

Carmen Ramirez brought in two cups of coffee and slices of marble pound cake.

"Thank you Carmen," said Marchand.

"This whole story started with Danny, abruptly leaving his part-time job of working security at a New York City Sports bar; he's a teacher. I don't know the reason he left, but after he did, the owner and his nephew were murdered in what was made out to be a robbery. If I get any more info from Tito, I'll let you know. But I think this kid, well he's not a kid at thirty-one, has stumbled upon some serious shit. You should also know that Danny's traveling with his girlfriend."

They shook hands and patted each other on the back.

"I'll get right on this," said Steinitz. He folded the paper with the numbers and slid them into his jacket pocket.

After he left, Marchand called Carmen into his office. "You can add Mr. Steinitz to the 'immediate access' list."

"You mean the list of 'one' that Mr. Lopez is on?" she said with a smile.

Marchand nodded twice and returned a smile.

❧ Chapter Thirty-Eight ❧

New Mexico

The narrow roads brought them through towns, the names of which, they couldn't pronounce.

"I'm hungry and I'm thirsty, how about you?" asked Kristen, breaking the silence.

They had just entered another small town, this one called, Candelaria, and before coming to the end of its major street, Danny noticed a luncheonette in the middle of empty store fronts.

"We'll stop here. I think we're safe; it's hard to track people who don't know where they're going. And for that matter, where is all that you eat going?"

She playfully slapped Danny and smiled. They both felt the tension that had been building, deflate.

Kristen was impressed with Danny's Spanish, as was the clerk who took their order of burgers and coke. Afterward they extended the relaxed tension by strolling around the town.

"We need a better plan than no plan," said Danny. He

walked out to the middle of the street and looked skyward, as if to receive some divine direction.

Kristen was reading a note stapled to a door which was written in both English and Spanish. Danny, who now was directing his attention to the town, saw Kristen reading the posted note and walked over to her.

"It says that the next time a priest will be here is August 31. That's about three and a half weeks from now. He must come once a month."

They held hands as they went past the adobe church. Danny playfully swung her arm, but then abruptly stopped.

"What Danny?"

"I've got an idea!" He led her back to the door with the note.

"Saint Michael's is going to get a priest earlier than expected," he announced.

❧ Chapter Thirty-Nine ❧

26 Federal Plaza, NYC – FBI Field Office
Steinitz knew his way around the building, and although retired, he still had access to most areas.

Assistant Director-In-Charge Nick Testa was waiting outside of his office. "Can't stay away, can you? You old coot!"

"I'd watch who you're calling 'old,' sonny."

They had been a good team, with the experienced Steinitz nurturing the young Agent, until he was ready to leave the nest. Testa credited his rise through the ranks, to his early training under Steinitz.

After shaking hands, Testa led Steinitz into his office, and closed the door.

"You sounded very urgent over the phone, so I take it that this is not a brisket and beer meeting."

"You're right, but that doesn't mean we couldn't partake afterwards; so I'll get right to the point. I need you to get me some information on a sitting US senator, 'Parsons' to be exact."

"Wow, you're aiming for the bulls eye right out of the gate. He's no small potatoes, he's 'Mr. America.'"

"Well I believe that he may be involved in some very un-American activities"

"I love it," said Testa. "I've been wanting to nail that son-of-a-bitch with his pants down. What do you have?"

"I take it that you've looked at him before?"

"Yes, but not lately."

"Well lately, some *things* have come up. I would like you to try again with some added ingredients – *I* can only go so far."

Steinitz placed a sheet of paper on Testa's desk.

"These numbers were given to me by another US senator, who got them from a NYPD cop. By the way, all of this is off the record."

Testa nodded.

"One of the New York numbers belongs to a, Frederick Shultz, remember that name?"

"Yes I do. That case is still open, even though the witnesses keep dying," said Testa.

"If you think there was an epidemic of *those* witnesses, that's nothing compared to the ones involved in the assassination of JFK," answered Steinitz.

Testa looked puzzled.

"I'll explain," said Steinitz. "Even as we were trying to get him deported for war crimes, he was working for, and against, the US government."

"For *and* against? Now I'm getting more confused. You're not drinking, are you?"

"When I get done we'll go out for that drink. It seems that elements from our own government, and some private citizens, were out to put an end to the JFK presidency. We always knew that Oswald didn't act alone, and we may now find out that he may not have acted at all. Parsons was too young to have been a part of it, but I got the telephone records, which shows phone calls from a 'Floyd Cooper' of Dallas, Texas to Shultz and Shultz to a Victor Strom. Years later, when our government decided to revisit the assassination, you might recall that I mentioned Strom to you as a possible shooter. We had placed him as being in Dallas on that fateful day. As I remember, you wanted to get on with current events and you weren't much interested in 'old stuff.' But then you changed your mind."

"Yes I did. And I remember the disappearing Mauser rifle. What do you want me to do?" asked Testa.

"I retrieved the phone numbers back and forth from Shultz to Cooper. Cooper to Parsons and Shultz to a guy named 'Posser.' This is where it really gets interesting. Posser, it seems, is connected to an organization called, 'Americans for God,' however it's with Parsons where I come up against a wall…..this is where you come in. I need to know where *his* calls go. I believe there is a perpetual group existing from 1963, and maybe even before, that runs in the background to our government. This is very scary stuff!"

"He doesn't have many friends in the Bureau, so I shouldn't have any problem," said Testa.

Steinitz looked pensive. "I'd rather you do this alone. If it turns out to become a large scale operation, then by all means, we'll call in the cavalry."

"I got it," said Testa.

"Okay, let's go for that brisket of beef, and of course, a brew," said Steinitz.

❧ Chapter Forty ❧

Candelaria, New Mexico

The Liberty was secured, out of sight, behind the church and against a back wall.

It was Friday morning, Danny's first day as a priest and Kristen's first role as Quasimodo, the bell ringer. She had volunteered to ring the steeple bells. There were two steeples in the front of the adobe church, and both had its own bell. All of Thursday was spent readying the church, which in Danny's eyes looked more like a chapel; cleaning, sweeping and putting in new candles. They hung notices around the town, which didn't take long, and talked it up at the lunch counter.

Father Dan McCoy greeted the sparse turnout, which was not a surprise. What was a surprise was that Kristen could play the organ. He had been told, that at one time, this was a thriving parish; one that was able to afford such a musical instrument.

Danny processed from the back of the church down the aisle and to the altar. It was just he and the alter boy; little Manny was the son of Irma, the luncheonette owner.

Danny held high, the *evangelistary*, and Manny hoisted a large crusafix. Father Dan greeted his congregation in both English and Spanish.

"My name is Father Dan McCoy, you may call me Father Dan. I'm in-between assignments and taking a vacation across our beautiful country. My sister Kristen, who played that beautiful piece by Mozart, as we processed in, is my traveling companion. In fact, it is my sister who saw the notice on your church door and convinced me to bring to you an important part of our faith. I don't know how long I'll be here, but I intend to have a daily mass for whatever period that is. So pass the word – all are welcome. Let it be known that all who have felt alienated in the past are welcome to attend. If anyone feels, for whatever reason, they should not receive the Eucharist, please see me after Mass. If you feel the love of Christ in your heart, you can approach the altar with that love. Saint Augustine guaranteed that!"

ॐ

"You never cease to amaze," said Kristen.

"And you too! Where did you learn how to play? I didn't see any piano in your apartment."

"That's because I couldn't afford one." Kristen quickly spoke again. "I'm sorry, that was short of me – that's the old Kristen who didn't learn to love." She placed her hand on Danny's.

"That's okay, you've earned that right, you don't have to apologize."

"I didn't earn anything, Danny. I certainly didn't deserve you. You're so good; maybe you missed your calling as a priest. I'm glad you did. But to answer your question about the piano, I learned to play after high school and during college. I didn't date…couldn't date, so I had plenty of time."

"When we get back, we'll have to get a piano," said Danny.

~

At the Friday morning Mass, the turnout was double that of Thursday. And Saturday's Mass was double that again. It was no secret that Danny's homilies were drawing in the numbers.

"No one here is a mistake," he began. "God doesn't make errors. We may be imperfect human beings, but our souls are born pure, and we have the free will to always change for the better. Unfortunately, some of us choose another direction. But none of us are born bad." Danny weaved in and out between English and Spanish. The transitions were smooth and seamless.

"So to repeat, no one here is a mistake, no one." Danny noted that nearly everyone received communion.

Each night Danny reviewed the missal for the next days Mass. After Friday's Mass, he began to break the hosts in quarters. Kristen thought that he was being too cautious, but after Saturday she could now see that their supply was dwindling.

"What are we going to do if tomorrow brings, more people to the altar then there are hosts? Where are we going to get unleavened bread or can you do the fishes and loaves too?" Kristen asked.

"I suppose we could use leavened bread, since we've broken a few other church laws, such as 'consecration' to name just one." Danny answered.

"Don't include me in this charade," said Kristen as she rummaged around in the Sacristy. She had found a cabinet behind the hanging vestments.

Danny stood watching as she disappeared behind the vestments and tried to pry open the cabinet. "At least I found an 'alb' that fit. I'm thankful for that," said Danny.

"And *I* just found a mother lode of hosts," announced Kristen. She crawled out from under the hanging wardrobe with two cases of hosts. "You won't have to be so cheap tomorrow."

"On that note, I'm going to call my brother Tito at his precinct." Tito's direct line was answered by someone else. Danny was told that Tito would be at work in an hour. The call was returned two hours later.

"Danny! It's great to hear your voice, man."

"I'm in New Mexico and I've run out of ideas. I can't stay doing what I'm doing. I know there are people working on the big picture, but now I need to feel safe and that can only happen if Kristen and I *are* safe."

"I hear you, and Dad is working on it. He is totally drawing on his old army buddies and he's getting in touch with a former helicopter pilot, who has his own plane. You can always call at this number and I'll get back to you."

"I will and say hello to everyone for us. Thanks Bro."

"Later Danny."

∾

The Sunday Mass was mobbed. It was as if a convention

had hit Candelaria; it had drawn people from other towns who heard of the "new priest of Candelaria." Besides little Manny, Father Dan now had a Lector. The procession, the music, the correct hand gestures and postures on the altar – it was not like those old movies of crooks disguised as clergy. But it was not the pageantry that drew them, it was the homilies.

Danny stood tall and confident.

"If you've come here to find God, you've come to the wrong place." This comment evoked murmurs throughout the congregation. "If you bring your faults through those church doors and not listen to the Word of God, then you might as well stay at home." More murmurs, but not as much as the first time. "But if you come here with an open heart, then you *will* experience a rush of love, so much so, that you will have to share it with others. If you let the church jump start your heart, love will follow, and all else will fall in place. As the Beatles once said, 'Love is all you need.' It is so true."

The rest of the Mass went well and full hosts were dispensed, not crumbs. The church was full to the brim or else Danny would have noticed a big tall man with a red beard standing with others in the back.

❧ CHAPTER FORTY-ONE ❧

Nick Testa did not waste his time after returning from lunch with Steinitz.

Senator Conrad Parsons had once approached Testa about "serving our country behind the scenes." He thought back to that day. At the time, he figured it to be a side job of looking for anti-Americans. He recalled that he had replied to Parsons, "that's what I already do," and left it at that. No further conversation took place and Testa had forgotten about it – until now. And only now did he realize that Parsons might have been talking about a nefarious outfit. *Maybe I'll soon find out.*

Although Steinitz had the knowledge and knew the ways to get at Parson's contacts, Testa had the means. In the morning, Testa put aside what he could and farmed out the rest to his team – he was on a mission. He used written logs, emails, telephone records, and actual leg work.

Cooper's name came up, as it did with Steinitz, but not as often as Supreme Court Justice Thomas Mann, or CIA Agent Mark Tolson. There were other senators and congressmen, and another Supreme Court Justice, but not as many hits or times availed to Thomas Mann. He would now check to see if any of these contacts were personal acquaintances outside of the Beltway. He would also check if any of the contacts in the Senate or the House were because of mutual projects.

At the end of the week he called Steinitz.

"I believe we have stumbled upon something, but I don't know what it is. There are numerous contacts with the same people, but it's not because of a social nature, and lots of contacts with other senators and congressman, without a social or project reason."

"What do you think?" asked Steinitz.

"We've gone about as far as we can go with lists and names. We need to listen," said Testa. "My suggestion is that you start with Thomas Mann," added Testa.

"We can't tap a Supreme Court Justice's phone, but I could put a device in his car," said Steinitz.

"That's just what I was thinking." Testa replied. "Maybe we'll get lucky."

"I'll do it," said Steinitz.

❧

Steinitz found that Mann took his private automobile back to his Virginia home each day. He could have been provided a chauffer, but liked to drive his own car.

Steinitz took the next plane out of La Guardia to D.C. The rain got heavier and the plane was buffeted with the wind. Normally Steinitz would have prayed that the rain stop, however, he wanted it to continue to add an element of cover.

Washington, D.C. was rain swept. The BMW was in a

secure lot; this he already knew. The guards were staying out of the rain and not doing their job. Steinitz could not have planned it any better, and was in and out of the car in seconds. Now he would wait.

Mann liked to exercise and walking to his car was part of his ritual. Steinitz was waiting across the street in his rental car. He would follow him to, and from his home, and keep this up until he had something; then he would remove the device.

Two days later, he removed the bug.

"What the hell are the *Apostles*?"

❧ Chapter Forty-Two ❧

Candelaria, New Mexico

The knock on the old pine door was strong. Danny heard it from upstairs, even with the downstairs shower going.

"Kristen could you get the door?" shouted Danny. The shower noise then registered. She had felt "sticky" after church, in the ninety degree heat – with no air conditioning and only one fan.

Danny bounded down the stairs, to the foyer; forgetting that his stay here was a form of witness protection. Expecting a parishioner, short of stature, he looked down as he opened the door, and into the man's broad chest. Danny's eyes rose until he was looking at eye level into a full faced, full bearded, and according to his designation on his collar a full fledged Bishop.

"Your Grace," said Danny. In a flash Danny had taken in his standing within the Church and showed proper respect. He looked to kiss his ring, but instead, the Bishop extended his hand.

"Shamus Muldoon," he declared.

"Dan McCoy," answered Danny.

"I apologize for barging in like this, but I was at the 9:00 Mass, here at Saint Mike's and wanted to meet you. You see, I'm the so called 'traveling priest' and the word got out that you were here before my time; a little play on words."

"A Bishop is a traveling priest?" *He had a jolly face*, Danny thought.

"During these times, the Church can't be choosey. I reached retirement age and this is now my *second* job, so to speak."

Danny noticed a little Irish lilt to his pronunciations.

"May I come in?" asked Muldoon.

"Oh sorry, I didn't realize we were still standing in the doorway."

Muldoon stepped through the foyer and past the vestibule into the living room.

"I take it you know my story?" said Danny. "I'm awaiting my first assignment and took this opportunity to travel across our vast country. My sister Kristen is traveling with me."

Just then Kristen came out of the bathroom door located between the kitchen and the living room. She was covered with a bath towel.

"Oh!" she exclaimed. "I didn't know we had company." Kristen hurried past the two men and went bare foot, up the stairs.

"That's my…" Danny was interrupted.

"Sister," Muldoon finished the sentence. "Is she being baptized today?"

Danny didn't know if this was a joke or not, so he ignored the question. "She can't take the heat as well as me, so, after being in that crowded church, she felt another shower would cool her off."

Muldoon didn't continue on this theme, but instead had other questions. "I understand you're changing some of the rules?"

"Maybe, but as you can see, if the church becomes inclusive, we can get the word out to a happier and larger audience. And let me add, I believe that Pope John the twenty-fourth will probably be going in that direction. All I did was to give it a little push. Why shouldn't every one participate in the Eucharist? Wife beaters and murderers who make a confession can receive the Eucharist, but a person married to a divorced person cannot? Makes no sense to me, I believe John the twenty-fourth is going to change all of that; including married priests."

"I agree with what you say, but rules are rules. That said, you're doing a great job. By the way what seminary did you attend?"

"The Immaculate Conception in Lloyds Neck on Long Island," Danny quickly answered. *So now come the questions – he's on to me.*

"How is Father Bob Martin doing?" asked Muldoon.

"Father Martin hasn't been there in ten years. He's Monsignor Martin now and is the pastor at Saint Dominic's in Oyster Bay, New York." *What a stroke of luck that was – knowledge gained from a chance meeting at a restaurant in Oyster Bay, Long Island.*

For the moment, Danny felt Muldoon was satisfied with his responses. And having Kristen join them and taking their order for coffee and tea helped to put aside the questions.

"Muldoon and McCoy, these are great Irish names, and you, Kristen?"

"McCoy, of course," answered Kristen, matter-of-factly.

"Yes, yes, yes, you're his sister," said Muldoon, seemingly correcting himself.

I guessed wrong, he's still skeptical, thought Danny.

Outside the weather had turned abruptly, from a hot August day to dark clouds with wind and rain. The prediction was that it would last into the night.

"You're welcome to stay here for the night?" said Danny. *And just think, you can ask more questions.*

"I'm going to take you up on that. My eyesight for night driving, isn't what it used to be."

"Great, let's go and get some dinner at Mary's, our only late night restaurant – good food and relaxed atmosphere."

When they got back from Mary's, Kristen took sheets from the linen closet, and made a bed out of the living room couch. She said her 'goodnights,' and went upstairs to retire for the night. Danny felt Muldoon had more to say. Danny sat on a chair and Muldoon sat on his newly made bed. Outside it had gotten worse.

At dinner, they were told that they could address him as Shamus. He said, "Your Grace" just doesn't cut it in a relaxed atmosphere.

"I believe you made a good decision, Shamus," said Danny. The howling wind put an exclamation point on his remark.

The two big men sat opposite each other.

"Dan, I so wish I didn't have to say this. You're so much better than so many priests, young or old that it's almost a disservice to the church that I have to ask you not to say Mass again. In fact it pains me."

"When did you know?" asked Danny.

"It was when you answered my question about the Seminary. In the last two years, there were only two seminarians each year. I knew the names of all four, because Father McElvoy, who is there now, was a classmate of mine. McCoy wasn't one of them. Did you have any training, any training at all?"

"None," said Danny. "As a little boy, I read everything I could about Catholicism. Devoured was probably more like it. I was adopted by a church going family – it's really a family of saints," added Danny as he thought about them.

Danny told him his story, but only of the events concerning the mob. Muldoon sat and listened. At times he shook his head in disbelief.

"I'll stay on," said Muldoon. "You and your 'sister' can stay too, until you sort out your next step. As for Saint Mike's, we can be on the altar, together, and you can do the homily. It will be my honor, Danny. I only wish there was a battle field commission on making priests."

"Thank you for that, Shamus."

They shook hands and said their goodnights.

∞

At 2:00 a.m. Kristen's cell phone rang and Danny answered. "Tito is that you?"

"Listen Danny, our Precinct phone system was compromised. The Captain is going ape shit. It's fixed now, but you have to be careful, we don't know who did it or for how long. Be very alert, Bro."

"I got it. I'll let you know what we decide." Danny hung up the phone.

"What?" Kristen asked.

"We're going to be on the move again. They might have traced earlier phone calls into the Precinct." Danny went over to his luggage, took out a blue case and snapped open its two latches. Five bullets were loaded into a snub nose .38 Special.

"Does this scare you?" asked Danny.

"No, I'm actually glad you have it."

"You never cease to amaze me too," said Danny.

❧ CHAPTER FORTY-THREE ❧

Posser watched the light from the second floor window go black. Before it was turned off, he saw Danny's face through the thin shade; he would wait another hour before breaking in and killing them both.

He waited beyond an hour and looked forward to be leaving his uncomfortable car seat. Posser sat up, and was about to make his move, when a phone rang, and the upstairs light went on again. *Shit what's going on, this was so perfect.* It stayed on for thirty minutes and then went off.

Posser's rental car was parked at Saint Michael's door. He was there through the storm and now waited, again, for their sleep to be his accomplice. Since the wind and the rain had left, the only movement in town was when Posser shifted his position, which he did often. He looked at his watch, it said 4 a.m. Now was the time.

The stillness was both his friend and his foe; it kept them asleep, but the slightest noise could also give him away. He opened the unlocked door, which gladly did not squeak.

"Who's that?" A voice from within the room asked.

Posser was startled by the voice of an older man with an

accent. He drew his knife and went past the stairs, following the voice into the room.

Muldoon rose up dragging his sheet with him. The flash of the blade was caught in the moonlight and Muldoon whipped the sheet at it. Posser didn't expect such a large mass rising out of the darkness. The knife and sheet became entwined.

"You fucking brigand!" shouted Muldoon.

"DANNY! WAKE UP! There's a fight or, something going on downstairs," exclaimed Kristen.

Danny bounded out of bed and went down the stairs, three at a time. Through the moonlight, he saw a white sheet swirling around two men, until one of them kicked high, sending the other into a heap. Danny faced the "Lugar Man," eye to eye.

Before Danny could react, he was kicked in the stomach. He reached for his .38, but it wasn't there. It had fallen out of his waistband on his way down. As he was being pummeled, Danny found the knife lying on the floor. Posser saw this and stepped on Danny's arm; a loud metallic sound then followed, as Posser fell forward and into the knife that Danny had retrieved; it went through his heart.

Kristen was still holding the iron fold-up chair. "I told you that I would be of help," she said through her tears.

They both went to Muldoon, who was dragging himself to his feet.

"I killed him, Shamus," said Danny, looking for absolution.

"God forgives you." Muldoon said quickly. "Now I want you to take my car and get away from here. I'll say that he broke in and he fell on his knife. My car is parked next to yours, it's slow but sure."

Danny shook his head no. "These are ruthless people, hiding a terrible secret, and I don't want you to get involved. If we take your car, they might figure that you know more than you should, and your life would be in danger. Right now you have no idea of what this is all about, so you can tell them the truth. We were here and now we're gone. I'm going to leave you some money in a draw upstairs, hide it – it's for you and the church. Don't use any of it until you hear from me. If that day doesn't come, destroy it all."

Muldoon looked puzzled, but nodded his head as if he understood.

"We have to leave right away. Someday we'll be able to return, and then we'll celebrate Mass together," said Danny.

Muldoon shook Danny's hand, he then held Kristen shoulders. "I'm Kristen Marks, Danny's friend," she said.

"Nice to meet you, Danny's friend," said Muldoon, his eyes twinkling.

After packing the Liberty, they said their final goodbyes.

"May God bless you both. And Danny, you are a better priest than I," said Muldoon.

"You got that from *Kipling*, and I consider it a great honor to be compared to Gunga Din," said Danny through a broad grin. The smile was returned.

Before they took off, Danny made a call, using Muldoon's cell phone, to his cousin in Albuquerque. They left with the gift of Muldoon's cell phone; in the same direction as its last call.

❧ CHAPTER FORTY-FOUR ❧

Washington D.C./Dallas, Texas

"Their man, 'Posser,' is dead, and now I believe is a good time to terminate that branch. What do you think?" asked Parsons.

Cooper was aware that this was more of a courtesy call, than asking for his advice. "I think you're right, they've served their purpose. And once again, this average citizen, has gotten the best of a, so called, highly trained soldier," said Cooper. "Maybe y'all will agree that this Lopez guy isn't so ordinary," he added.

"It's done then. I'll call the job in," said Parsons. He had already given the order an hour before he called Cooper.

"Good," answered Cooper. *He's probably already done this, and they're probably, already dead*, thought Cooper.

After the call, Cooper reflected back to other times when all the pieces had come together to pull off the greatest spoof in American history. Shultz and Strom were two old men now, but at one time they were a very important part of our picture. He then wondered, when, it would be decided by Parsons, that *his* piece of the puzzle would be terminated.

❧ CHAPTER FORTY-FIVE ❧

26 Federal Plaza, NYC – FBI Field Office
Nick Testa's secure line rang.

"Dick, I'm glad you called, I got some updates on our mutual project," said Testa. "But it's your call, so you go first."

"Danny's on the move," said Steinitz. "I just heard from his brother, the NYPD cop, and he tells me that Danny had to leave his church hide-a-way. The same fake highway patrolman showed up again. There was a fight, and 'Eric Posser' is no longer with us. I understand it was a joint operation – three against one. They'll send in the CIA next, and the results won't be so positive. That's my story, what do you have?" asked Steinitz.

Testa cleared his throat. "My surveillance has thrown a brighter light on your initial discovery of the *Apostles*. The word is being used as if it's some secret sect, but worse yet, maybe an additional government body. The *Apostles* seem to have woven themselves throughout our society. Although we couldn't tap into the lines of the major players, like Parsons, we were able to backtrack and pick up this info from phone records, and listening in on those supporting players."

"You are saying *we*, I thought we agreed……." Steinitz was interrupted.

"I'm sorry, Dick, this has become more than a simple hide and seek operation, and I couldn't do it alone. I'm using agents spread throughout the Bureau, who have been my closest, trusted, friends for years and see the world the way *we* see it. It's not like, 'calling in the cavalry,' not just yet. What you've uncovered by bugging Mann's car, could be a clue to the most important threat our country has ever faced. And the irony is that it's from the very people that proclaim themselves to be patriots. The fact that you also found out that, 'Mister God Fearing Supreme Court Justice Thomas Mann' has a girlfriend is juicy, but that's not what we're about." He paused, "I have something else – Shultz and Strom are dead. Frederick Shultz was found in his car, shot to death, and a Star of David was painted on his forehead. Victor Strom was found dead in his apartment due to a faulty gas stove. All in a three hour time frame – shades of 1963. I don't believe either death is what is seems," said Testa.

"Is there any way that you could help Danny?" asked Steinitz.

"If we did, then they would know that we're on to them. I don't want to leave him dangling out there, but if he could elude them for a little while longer – just to give us more time to gather evidence."

"'A little while longer' is too weak to hang your hat on. The Lopez family is very resourceful, and as you can see, Danny is no slouch in the hero department," said Steinitz.

"What we can do, is turn a blind eye on how you extract him. We certainly want to hear what he has to say, but we can't show our hand, just yet," said Testa.

"I understand and I'll keep in touch," said Steinitz.

❧ Chapter Forty-Six ❧

Washington, D.C.

The three month old proposal of an amendment to the United States Constitution, by two of the most conservative representatives and senators in congress, was not unusual, but what they did propose was startling. The proposal was to repeal the second amendment and replace it with a ban on all hand guns, and a re-registration of all long guns, but for only licensed hunters. The federal 'Collector of Curios and Relics' license would be revoked along with all state licenses. All rifles and hand guns would be turned into the local police departments, where documents on them were kept. In order to placate the hunters, wording was inserted into the amendment that stated, 'a return of long guns upon the issuing of new hunting licenses.' Both congressmen had just been elected in the prior year and were in no danger of losing their seat. The Liberals were ecstatic and Parsons was publicly livid, but behind the scenes his top aide worked to pass the proposal.

In a controlled and decisive tone, he was speaking to his

aide, Jeffrey Mann, the thirty year old son of the Supreme Court justice.

"Jeff, you tell Senator James, that natty Republican, that if he doesn't vote yes on this amendment, his girl friend will be very unhappy, not to mention his wife. And tell that fucking cowboy, Senator John Wright, that knowledge of his boyfriend, might not go over too well among his red necked constituency. And for good measure, let's get Senator Marshall Adams on board by sharing with him the video we have of him, his wife and their Swedish nanny – complete with audio. That ought to put an exclamation mark on his so called revolutionary lineage. These votes, all of the *Apostles*, and practically all of the Democrats, along with cheering from an anti-gun president, should ride this proposal all the way to ratification. We're getting close to preserving our country's values. General Spencer Thompson is with us, as is Generals Smythe and Koss. We must not let our country fall to the elitists and do-gooders. They're no good commies and we'll deal with them once we have succeeded."

"And you'll be the lone voice of freedom, rising against the liberal tide," said Mann.

"That's right Jeff; we will finally finish what was started before we were born. The good news is the Liberals think that *they've* won. Hitler had it right, take away their guns and there won't be any Revolutionary War. And someone said that it couldn't happen here." Parson gave a short laugh, "ha," and Mann smiled.

After Jeffrey Mann stepped out of the office, Parsons called Agent Mark Tolson.

"What do you have?" asked Parsons. "Do you have anything more on what happened with Schultz's man?"

"Well they're no longer in Candelaria. According to the local cops, this Posser character caught it in a church rectory two days ago. A Bishop, who was sleeping downstairs, says someone attacked him during the night, and he was knocked unconscious. He said he is just here 'making his rounds.' He said that when he regained consciousness, the nice young visiting priest and his sister were gone and Posser was dead. I checked the Bishop out, he's legitimate. Of course the young priest would be our boy."

"You keep in touch and use any means you want to put an end to Lopez," said Parsons.

❧ CHAPTER FORTY-SEVEN ❧

Albuquerque, New Mexico

Danny and Kristen had managed to fit her clothes and traveling goods into one very heavy suitcase and "the rest of your 'necessities' you squeezed into *my* suite case," Danny had said.

He dropped Kristen off at the Greyhound Bus Station, on 1st Street.

"Take my Yankee hat, even if it kills you, and tuck your hair into it. My cousin has us booked into the Holiday Inn in Amarillo, under the name of Preston. That's his new wife's name and the hotel has a credit card with that name on file. Stay put and don't go out; eat all of your meals at the hotel and have them charge it to that card, every time. I will catch up with you. When you get to the bus station in Amarillo, go two blocks south; there are no cameras at that point. My cousin has a friend who will take you to the hotel. He'll be in a red pick-up truck. If by some chance I don't make it to Amarillo, stay at the hotel and Tito will come for you."

They hugged outside of the car. Danny had to pry her

arms off of his neck. Each said, "I love you," twice, before Danny got back into the Liberty and drove off. *At least she is safe.*

Two hours later, Kristen took the 10:35 a.m. bus to Amarillo.

∾

Danny waited for dark, and after 12 midnight, parked the Liberty for the final time, by a Fire Department decorated with a colorful mural. He checked out his ride, tapped the Liberty on its hood and said, "Well done." Danny carried the heavy suite case for one block, turned, and went down a dead-end street. In the dark, away from the dim lighting he saw the red pick-up truck.

❧ CHAPTER FORTY-EIGHT ❧

Washington, D.C.

"Unbelievable! Unbelievable!" Parsons kept repeating. "It flew through both houses and went through three-fourths of the states legislatures in about the same time. I can't believe it! It's like changing the Ten Commandments."

"The state legislatures went against the will of many of their constituents," said Jeffrey Mann.

"It's the law now, and they can't do a fucking thing about it," said Parsons.

"Those same 'fucking people' are calling on you to run for president. Meanwhile, *the* President has sent out the word for all police chiefs to begin to round up all hand guns and all long guns."

"Yeah I know," said Parsons. "It was the doing of some of our most conservative legislatures who did the work to pass this amendment. The Liberals and many Democrats sat back with open mouths not making a sound, and watched it happen, what they had wanted all along – spearheaded by the opposing party. Our guys even wrote the rules of play, a ten thousand dollar fine for not turning in your gun or guns and five years in jail. Up to a five hundred dollar credit on your tax return based on the fair market value of the hand gun being turned in. Nothing for a long gun, because it was assumed that a hunting application would return it to them." Parsons sat back in his desk chair and processed what he had just told Mann.

He continued, "I want you to start the procedures for me to run for president. Notify the press and other media."

Mann left the office on a mission.

"Parsons, again, sat back in his chair. 'Parsons for President' he said aloud. "It has a nice ring to it, but it will never happen."

∾

Parson's phone rang. He noted the ID and answered without a hello.

"My team found the black Liberty parked by a large mural, decorating a fire station in Albuquerque. I'm on my way there now," said Tolson.

Parson's nodded his head and spoke into the receiver, "Good."

❦ CHAPTER FORTY-NINE ❦

Amarillo, Texas

Danny knocked on room 24A. He listened for any movement to come from the other side of the door. He knocked again, and again – not a foot step, not a sound. Danny cupped is hands against the door and spoke into them. "I didn't know we had any knocking signal?"

This time he heard running feet and latches being unhooked, before the door flung open. Danny was greeted the same way as when they departed, with a headlock. He held her close, with his arms crossed behind her back and around her tiny waist; her arms held him tightly around his neck.

❧ CHAPTER FIFTY ❧

New York, NY/Washington, DC

Richard Steinitz stared at his computer screen, "THE SECOND AMENDMENT IS GONE." Under this headline was something else that was startling, "Parsons For President," followed by "Long Live Parsons." *Almost the entire Republican Party, all of the Conservatives and many moderate Democrats, especially gun owners, want him to skip the election process and proceed to what? A King, an Emperor, The Fuhrer?* Steinitz shuddered. He called Marchand's office.

Before Steinitz could speak into the receiver, Marchand responded, "I'm not surprised."

"What happens next?" asked Steinitz.

"I voted against this amendment and against what *my* constituency wanted. Notices here, in New York, have gone out. My hand gun is to be turned in by the end of the week. It's worth fifteen hundred, but I'll receive a credit on my tax return of five hundred dollars. Who gets this gun? Nobody knows." Marchand continued. "The liberal press here in New York is in ecstasy. They think this is *their* victory. I think it's their defeat. Before the vote, I was called by, what I believe was a low level operative of Parsons, to vote *for* this amendment. When I told him that I wouldn't do it, he didn't defend his position, he just said okay."

"That's strange that someone from Parson's office would be campaigning *for* this amendment?" said Steinitz.

"That is strange, but stranger yet, is the strong arm tactics used on other fellow Republican congressmen. A Republican congressman who knows my views on Roe v Wade and gay marriage, confided in me that he is gay and that this fact was thrown up to him by the same gentlemen who called me. It was either vote for this or be 'outed.' Before you ask me why? I believe I know why. *They* want us unarmed. And I shudder to guess that the even bigger plan might be to take control of our government."

"Holy shit!" was Steinitz response.

"What Danny Lopez uncovered was not, *just* the assassination truths, but an ongoing plot to eventually take over our country. We must do all we can to protect Danny and to protect our way of life. Right now this group is stronger and more organized than us; our strength lies in the fact that they don't know that we're on to them. If they did, we would be dead."

❧ CHAPTER FIFTY-ONE ❧

Amarillo, Texas/Washington, D.C.

Parson's secure line sounded and a CIA number was displayed.

Parson barked into the receiver, "You better have something positive to tell me Agent Tolson."

Parsons', emphasized, formal tone, put Tolson on the defensive.

"Their car, Sir, was both cleaned out and 'clean.' Nothing could be gotten from it, but we are checking the surveillance cameras in the City, and all roads leading out of Albuquerque. I have twenty trusted men here, and in Amarillo, going over the data. We can enhance the images and get right into the vehicle to see if they shaved that day or didn't put on their make-up. So far, what the cameras have given us, is that Kristen Marks boarded a bus to Amarillo. It shows her arriving and leaving the bus depot in Amarillo, carrying a suitcase. The cameras follow her for two blocks and when their surveillance coverage ends, she disappears. The camera outside of the fire station in Albuquerque, gives us Danny Lopez leaving his parked car and walking away, carrying a large suitcase. It's midnight, but he can still be identified. When the surveillance runs out, he too, disappears, this time into the dark. It looks as if they have split up, but I wouldn't rule out a re-connect." Tolson thought he was very thorough, but still braced himself for Parson's customary response.

Parsons was livid. "This is unacceptable, I want every fucking camera, both in Albuquerque and Amarillo scrutinized. I don't care how many men it takes or where you get them from. Use every resource. Tell the ones who are not *Apostles* that you're looking for terrorists." Parson's voice cracked through the receiver as Tolson held it away from his ear.

"Sir I will do my best. The woman left at the height of traffic. As for Lopez, a little after midnight, there was a power outage in Albuquerque, so our best bet is with the woman. I'll pull all the tapes and disks from every camera that I can find. I'm working out of two storefronts, one in Albuquerque and one in Amarillo. I'm sure she's still in Amarillo; Lopez could have gone in any direction. My focus is on the woman. Find her and we'll get him too. And besides that, she's an easier target. I'll get more men from McLean."

Parson needed Tolson's drawn out rhetoric to calm his own psyche; realizing that their plot was coming to fruition, and that Tolson was an important player.

"Good, get on it Mark, this problem needs to be solved and then we can move on to bigger and better things. On that note, how are you doing with Dallas?"

"I sent two men there yesterday. I told them not to call, but to report to me in person," said Tolson. *That's the first time in a long time he's used my first name. Maybe he's remembered that he personally picked me to be recruited by the Apostles, and that since then, I've been responsible for many Agents to join.*

"Good! It sounds like you have things under control," said Parsons, before ending their conversation.

He called Jeffrey Mann into his office.

"Jeff, our adjunct tentacle in Texas has been taken care of. Their knowledge was dangerous and they had outlived their usefulness. As we speak, their final curtain is coming down."

Jeffrey Mann smiled to himself, as Parsons' speech making sometime entered into normal conversation.

∽

Dallas, Texas

If Colonel Floyd Cooper were waiting at his front entrance he would have seen a trail of billowing dust approaching, followed by a second cloud of dust.

Kincaid parked his Mercedes in the circular driveway and entered through the unlocked large cone shaped front doors.

"COOPER?" Kincaid called out. He walked up the winding staircase to where he believed the voices were coming from. Kincaid was too preoccupied with straining his weak hearing to have heard the arrival of the second car which parked behind his Mercedes. Two men got out.

"COOPER?" Kincaid called out, again. As he approached a door, the sounds became clear to his faulty hearing. It was not a conversation, but grunts along with higher pitched moans. The clarity came too late, as Kincaid was already into the room. Cooper looked up from his prone position.

"What the fuck?"

"You sent word that you wanted to see me," said Kincaid, in a soft voice.

The woman screamed as two men entered the room.

The next day, the Dallas Times ran two large obituaries proclaiming the sudden death of two of its most prominent businessmen, and founders for many years of charitable projects in the Dallas area. It noted they had died from a faulty gas stove. No mention was made of the woman.

❧ Chapter Fifty-Two ❧

Amarillo, Texas

The store front was a crowded scene of computer screens and discarded coffee cups, strewn into overflowing waste baskets.

Lawrence Trasker looked again at the image on the screen. His bleary eyes strained to focus. Kristen Marks' picture lay on his desk looking up at him, as he made the screen define the passenger in the red truck. It was her. He pulled the memory stick from the USB port.

When the agents first arrived, their first step was to locate all of the surveillance systems, both commercial and private, and copy their content onto a removable device. Fortunately the systems were high-end and had USB ports for copying evidence. The next step was to label the systems by route, a simple 1-2-3. The Albuquerque group was numbered 1-2-3 in ascending order of leaving that city. The Amarillo systems were labeled 3-2-1, in descending order, reflecting traffic coming into the city. Each camera was given a letter route to go along with their numbered sequence.

Trasker was looking at route C on surveillance camera

number one. It was the last in the sequence, and the one which showed Kristen, in the red pick-up, going in the direction of the Holiday Inn. Trasker took memory sticks, numbers one, two, three and four and shoved them into his pocket. He then announced that he was taking a lunch break. Numbers five and above had been assigned to another agent. Instead of going to the local fast food place, Trasker took the CIA rented car and went to the surveillance center running the C sequence, camera number one.

He introduced himself as he flashed his credentials.

"It seems that our copies are not working," he announced to the staff of two. With their permission, he took the CD-R disks for that time period, and while, again, waving his CIA I.D., he removed the hard drive. "We'll review these and bring them back tomorrow."

"Take your time sir, before you walk out the door, my boys will have another hard drive installed."

Trasker saw a sign in a stationery store which advertised its fax and shredding services, but decided the less involved the better. After stomping on the memory sticks and hard drive, he threw them into a street drain. He scraped the disks until they were raw and threw them into a second drain. The rental car was left in front of the stationery store. Trasker took out his cell phone and called Testa.

"I got lucky; I was given the surveillance data with the Marks girl on it."

"Good work Larry," said Testa. "Now 'get out of Dodge,' you've done what we hoped you could do. Its time, again, for you to return to being a Special Agent. Don't use a car, it's too far to drive and it gives them too much time to intercept you. Safe home."

On the trip into Amarillo, Trasker recalled seeing a charter bus service. He hoofed it there, quick time, for about five city blocks.

"We have a charter leaving in about thirty minutes to Oklahoma City," said the driver, who also seemed to be the owner.

"I'll wait," said Trasker, who was sweating profusely. *This is not dry heat, it's hot heat.*

"I GOT HER!" An agent yelled out. Immediately, everyone stopped their search and went to this agents screen. He was working on route C memory stick number five. A call went out to the Albuquerque group to look for a red pick-up truck.

"Who has the next numbered down memory stick?" asked Tolson.

"Trasker," was simultaneously shouted out. "Numbers one, two, three and four are missing."

"Where is he?" asked Tolson.

"He went to lunch," said an agent who worked on the desk next to Trasker.

"It's now 4 p.m." Tolson pointed at four agents, "You, you, you and you, come with me."

They found the rented car five blocks away. "I know he's not walking," said Tolson as his cell phone went off.

"We called over to the company running the surveillance center, and explained that we were coming over to pick up the backup disks, but they said one of our men had already been there and took them. Not only that, he pulled out their hard drive," said the agent on the cell call.

"Shit! He's a fucking mole, probably the FBI. They haven't

trusted us since Kennedy," said Tolson. "This is important," he added, "I don't want him dead!"

Tolson had his men spread out in four different directions from where the rental car was parked. Being connected by cell phones, it wasn't long before Tolson heard his distinct ring.

"I think we have his escape route. I'm at a small charter bus company, and the son of the owner says that his father took off with a run to Oklahoma City about a half hour ago. One of the passengers matches Trasker's description."

Tolson called his men back to the rented store front. "You three take one of our staff cars and intercept that bus. Remember I want him alive," repeated Tolson.

Even though the bus had a half hour jump on them, the three man team hit speeds in excess of one hundred miles per hour. Their flashing lights chased out of their way, cars traveling at eighty miles per hour.

One of the men called out. "There it is!"

They pulled in front of the bus with lights still flashing and now added a siren.

Trasker knew they were here for him. He reached under his suit jacket for his 9mm, but halted midway as a two year old boy being held by his mother in the seat in front of him, turned back, and gave him a big smile.

The door of the bus opened and Trasker got up, raised his hand as a gesture of compliance, and moved to the door. He had made up his mind, that his duty to his country was primary. He had not married and was not in any relationship. His job with the FBI *was* his life. As he walked to the front of the bus, he thought of how many heroes did the right thing regardless of the outcome. He would think no more.

The door closed on the bus and dust created by its acceleration, plus the noise of its loud engine covered up Trasker's 9mm being drawn. *If they thought it was over, they got the wrong guy*, he thought.

He shot the first one in the temple, the second one in the chest. The third agent shot him in the stomach. As he was falling, Trasker leveled his gun at the agent, but was shot a second time ending his life.

Tolson was not happy with the news. However, he understood, and told the agent who shot Trasker that he was putting him in for a commendation.

"What do we have so far on the red pick-up? Do we have a license?" asked Tolson.

"Sir, the red truck, is a dirty red truck. The plate can't be read, but we can identify it as a New Mexico plate. We're checking all registered trucks of that color, make and model."

"I want you to check the registrations for the last five years. Just in case he might have *forgotten* to re-register. In fact, now that I'm thinking about it, check the delinquent registrations first. That dirty plate might be telling us more than meets the eye. No pun intended."

"Yes sir, I will."

❧ CHAPTER FIFTY-THREE ❧

Washington, D.C.

Marchand's intercom came alive as Carmen announced that Richard Steinitz was on his private line.

"Dick, I was going to call *you*" said Marchand, speaking first.

"I'll cut to the chase," answered Steinitz. "We have to extract Danny and Kristen – and sooner than later. As you know I've been working with my former partner who's now the Assistant Director in New York, and he's being told the CIA has an all out search and destroy mission going on in the Southwest, probably for Danny. The FBI has a man planted with them, but the only thing he could do is hold them up for one or two days. And finally, when they are able to I.D. Danny and Kristen, they'll also be able to I.D. the driver who took them to the hotel. What can we do?"

"The driver is a friend of a Lopez cousin. I'll call Tito and let him know," said Marchand.

There was a pause and then Marchand spoke again.

"I don't know if this piece of news is adding to the suspense or maybe it's a mystery all on its own."

"Okay, I'm listening," said Steinitz.

"In today's New York Times there is a small article announcing major troop re-assignments. The 22nd Mechanized Division is moving from Fort Hood, Texas to Fort Bragg, North Carolina."

"Fort Bragg? Isn't that the home of the 82nd Airborne Division, like forever?" asked Steinitz.

"Very good Dick, you know your military posts. But listen it gets intriguing. At the same time it is reported that the 82nd Airborne Division will be moving to Fort Dix, New Jersey. It says that their access to the air field at McGuire will be a 'big plus.' It was presented as if the benefit was for the 82nd. But I think this move was for the purpose of the 22nd Mechanized Division, and that they couldn't care less where the 82nd Airborne went. So far no intrigue, except for the missing ingredient that the 22nd is under the command of Major General Spencer Thompson."

"Senator Parsons' best buddy," said Steinitz.

Marchand paused before speaking, "And now the question is why? Because it's a closer route to Washington? I shudder to think the unthinkable, which is a military take-over of our country. If logic has it, then this would be in the natural order of events. The taking of guns from private citizens, a leader – Parsons, who says he will return them, his rise to power by saying one thing, but having his own agenda and finally a majority of the military backing him. Scary stuff and they said it could never happen here."

"Holy shit!' exclaimed Steinitz, for the second time.

"I'll call Tito and get back to you," said Marchand.

The phone call ended with Marchand immediately hitting the speed dialer with Hector's name.

∾

Amarillo, Texas

Muldoon's borrowed cell phone blared out Wagner's *Valkyrie*, breaking the silence, and startling Danny and Kristen. The conversation ended with Danny saying, "I understand."

"What is it?" asked Kristen.

"That call was from Tito. He said to 'get out,' meaning leave the hotel. He said that he's coming for us and we're to leave and head in a direction south of here, but not more than one hundred miles. He'll let us know where the exact pick up point will be. One of Dad's friends will be flying us out."

"Thank God for Dad's friends," said Kristen.

∾

New Mexico

David Redpath was warned. His small home stood in the middle of a clearing; a dirt road came out of a line of trees leading up to the front door of the weathered clapboard cabin. The red pick-up was parked along side between the house and the barn.

"If they come, I'll be ready for them," he told Tito. "I'll be awake, not like my Cheyenne brothers were when Lt. Col. George Armstrong 'fucking' Custer led a charge into a camp of sleeping women and children."

"They need information from you about Danny, so at first they'll want to talk," said Tito.

"At first," Redpath repeated, "But this Indian isn't going to play by their rules. I'm not giving up Danny and Kristen, and *this cavalry* is not going to do as they please – not this time."

Redpath scoped out his home to come up with the best defense. He sent his wife and their twin daughters to her sister's house, but kept his two teenaged sons with him. He had one shotgun, two lever action rifles and one bolt action rifle, no automatic or semi-automatic guns. They did, however, have keen hearing and all of the Redpath's were crack shots.

∾

Cape Cod, Massachusetts

"I heard that you would be calling, man. Man it was so good to hear your father's voice. Its been a long time. I told him that I will do anything to help him."

Coleman Mays had been a medevac chopper pilot in Vietnam. When Hector was awarded the Medal of Honor, Hector spoke and said that half of this medal should go to a Lieutenant Mays. No one knew who Mays was.

Most of his friends called him Cole, as did Hector, but he was sometimes called Willie. His mother had named him after a famous tenor saxophone player named Coleman Hawkins.

"I'm leaving tomorrow morning, how long should it take?" asked Tito.

"About four hours without stopping," said Mays. He explained the Airpark set-up and how Tito would find him.

"If you have any weapons, it might be a good idea to pack them." said Tito.

"I'm ready to lock and load," said Mays.

I guess that means he has some, thought Tito. "Okay, see you bright and early tomorrow," he said.

∽

Tolson had news, and he knew that Parsons' mood reflected on whether it was good or bad. He decided that, even though it was good, he would still use a formal approach.

"Sir, we have intercepted two phone calls of interest. The first one is a call from Tito Lopez to Hector Lopez. The father basically says that he has a plan to bring his son Danny back from Texas. He asked Tito to meet him tonight at the family home. The next call was from Hector Lopez to a Coleman Mays in Massachusetts. From what I got out of the conversation between Lopez and Mays, who lives on Cape Cod, is that they're putting together some kind of a rescue mission. I got the *skinny* on this Mays; he's a former chopper pilot that served with Lopez in Vietnam. He might own a small plane, and this may be our best way of finding Lopez' son Danny. We'll let him lead us to them."

Parsons listened and liked what he heard.

"Wherever they lead us to, I want them all dead and they can stay and rot where they fall. They're the last piece of old business, and the last link to the death of Camelot. Put an agent on Tito."

Tolson did not understand the reference to Camelot, nor did Parsons believe that he would. In a way, he was talking to himself.

❧ Chapter Fifty-Four ❧

New Mexico

It could have been a scene out of an old western, except that it was Indians inside a cabin, that were being attacked, and the attackers came in by car instead of by horse.

"I see them, Daddy," Redpath's number one son exclaimed.

"We have the advantage of them wanting to question us, so in the beginning, they will not shoot to kill. After they get what they want, it'll be back to, 'the only good Indian is a dead one,'" *Some things never change*, thought Redpath.

The dirt road wound around through what seemed to be the only vegetation in the area. It was an oasis within a desert like terrain, finally ending at a line of trees; leaving fifty yards of open space to a small cabin.

"What do you think, should we leave the car here at the edge, or should we move forward with it?" asked one of the agents, from the back seat.

"It's too open," the one in charge answered. "Go *real* slow," he said to the driver, "and when you get to the barn, gun it and park on the side away from the house." He pointed out the direction.

"They're angling away from the house toward the barn," said Redpath. "We'll let them get a little closer, and on three, take out the tires, and then we'll see what their next plan is."

"Two...three." A barrage of gun fire erupted from the house. The car braked and the occupants ducked. The smooth shooting 30cal. lever action rifles made short work of the two front tires and caused the engine to discharge most of its fluids; smoke filled the air.

"We can't stay here," the agent in the back stated, "maybe we should call for assistance?"

"No, we can do this job without any help," said the agent in charge.

"You're risking our lives, sir."

"You shut the fuck up or I'll put you on report."

The argument was intense and all three agents, with their heads lowered below the windshield, were voicing their opinions and were totally involved, until they heard a gentle tapping on the car windshield. As the thick smoke from the engine turned into wisps of white vapors, their arguing came to a abrupt halt; looking out, they saw three rifles pointing into the car. Redpath tapped again with the barrel of his shotgun, this time, motioning them to get out of their vehicle.

❧ CHAPTER FIFTY-FIVE ❧

Texas – South of Amarillo

Danny and Kristen, quickly and quietly, moved out of the hotel; having no fear of hiding their identity, Kristen's credit card was used to rent a car. They followed the instructions and headed south.

After traveling close to fifty miles, due south, they came upon a sign advertising cabins for rent. The cabins were off of the main road, and they chose the furthest one from the road.

"Perfect," said Danny. He checked the cell phone reception – it was good.

Kristen began to clean what she could.

"The bed is gross, I can't sleep on those sticky sheets, and god knows what the mattress is like?" she said.

"I totally agree, we'll sleep in the car," said Danny. "What do we have to eat?"

"We have just what I took from breakfast this morning. Six little boxes of cereal, no milk, and two bananas and an orange," said Kristen.

"I noticed that you said 'I' does that mean *I* have to beg?"

"Well that would be different," she said, curtly.

Danny went to throw her on the bed.

"NO BED! NO BED!" she screamed.

"Then it's the car."

"Okay," she feigned surrender, but was the first one out of the door; grabbing a bath towel on the way. "Not sticky," she added.

The back seat of the Japanese compact car could not accommodate Danny's legs so the door had to stay open. Over the last few days, stress had eliminated any desires. Danny's pent up craving was quickly fulfilled, but he continued at the same pace until Kristen called out her pleasure. She looked over Danny's muscular shoulders, at his legs dangling out of the door, and one pleasure was replaced by another. Kristen's smile complete with her tongue between her front teeth started her giggles.

ᑎᗩ

Washington, D.C.

Steinitz had traveled to Washington and was led into Marchand's office by Carmen. They shook hands which turned into a bear hug.

"Duke, it's good to see you, man," said Steinitz. "I have just about had enough of the telephone."

"Me too," said Marchand.

"Where are they" asked Marchand.

"I'm assuming they're in some local roach motel. Some place south of Amarillo, awaiting our call. I'm assuming this, because there's not much south of Amarillo. Danny's smart, he knows that hiding in less, will draw the least attention," answered Steinitz.

❧ CHAPTER FIFTY-SIX ❧

After long delays due to multiple accidents on the Long Island Expressway, Tito made it over the Throgs Neck Bridge. He took note of the overhead signs as to where the EZ Pass was accepted, but the heavy traffic had steered him over to the cash only lanes; seeing an opening, he abruptly cut his wheels, left, over to the EZ Pass lanes. Behind him, a blue Buick did the same. Tito was aware that he might be followed so he purposely repeated this action on the next toll before Connecticut, and again, the Buick made the same maneuver. His cell phone rang, it was Mario.

"Tito where are you?"

"I'm on my way to Cape Cod on a rescue mission for Danny; I'll explain when I have more time. What's up bro?"

"Dad is missing. Mom is frantic, it's not like him. As he left, he told her not to worry, but that there was something he had to take care of. Our family is turning into its own covert operation."

"What's your take on it," asked Tito.

"The only thing that I can think of is that it has something to do with what he's been reading, I should say devouring; newspaper reports about a proposed march on Washington, D.C. – this time by our own army. The Conservative Press says that it *should* be done and the Liberal press is clamoring for sanctions. The President says that, 'you can't sanction third party thinking.' I thought he was a war hero?"

"He is a hero, maybe like Dad, a quiet hero. I did see this stuff in the paper, but I wrote if off as just politics. I didn't know that my family was getting in deep with it," said Tito, "Anything else, before I have to break off?"

"Since you haven't read these reports, I'll quickly bring you up to date as to Dad's thinking. He feels that the real reason for moving the 82nd Airborne out of Fort Bragg, and the 22nd Mechanized Division under the command of General Spencer Thompson in, was to move the 22nd closer. Dad says he's a hawk of the worst kind. He says if this happens, it will be the end of our country, as we know it. He was sick over this, and now he's gone," said Mario.

"To me it sounds like Dad's okay. He left on his own and on a mission. You see to Mom and I'll get Danny back. Soon we'll be back to Sunday dinners," Tito said.

"Okay, I'll try and calm Mom down, and what is it, again, you're doing by going to Cape Cod?"

"I can't say too much, but it's the right thing to do. Meanwhile I've got some asshole on my tail – not said to be funny. I have an idea on how to lose him, and hopefully, he's never been to The Cape. Take care of the home front."

The Buick stayed with him as he drove over the Bourne Bridge, into the traffic circle, and took the exit for Hyannis. Commenting aloud on the Buick's traffic rotary skills, "Nice and smooth for a rookie," said Tito.

"You're right, he looks like he's headed for Hyannis Airport," said the Agent in the Buick, speaking into his cell phone.

"Good work," said Tolson. "Stay with him, I want to know the type of plane and its flight plan."

Tito took route six and got off at the Hyannis exit. As he approached the airport, there was one more traffic circle to complete. "Let's see what you can do with this one," said Tito, aloud.

Tito entered the rotary and purposely stayed to the inside, the Buick did the same. He went around twice, all of the time watching through his rear view mirror. Tito smiled, *he has to follow me. I could go around ten times.* His smile grew wider. Tito stayed to the inside as traffic built up in the outside lanes. As he came to route 132, before a Wendy's, he gunned his car, cutting off the outside traffic.

The Buick which was still in the inside lane, and because of the driver's lack of experience with rotaries, had to go around one more time, before following; merging to the outside and going after Tito.

Tito put distance between him and the rotary, and far enough down route 132 before turning left and circling around the back of stores in order to reach Route 28. As he made his turn on to route 28 toward Falmouth, he kept looking in his mirror for the Buick. Tito didn't have a plan if the Buick had followed, but it was nowhere in sight as he set course for the Falmouth Airpark.

"I lost him," said the Agent.

"You fucking what?" said Tolson. He paused, "Okay, now listen. He has to go back to the Hyannis Airport, so stake it out until you hear otherwise."

∞

The Agent's cell phone went off.

"Get your ass over to the Falmouth Airpark. It's where Mays, the pilot, keeps his plane."

Tolson had checked the FAA data base.

∞

Mays was screaming in his sleep, "I can't put it down, it's too hot, I can't put it down!" And then the futility took over. "Motherfucking, fucking piece of shit, fucking motherfucking war. They're going to die and it's going to be my fault," he cried. "I'm afraid, I can't land. No, no, please don't let this fucking happen, oh God please," he was sobbing.

Mays woke up to a bright sunny Cape Cod day. He had sweated through his tee shirt and shorts; his bottom sheet was soaked. During his time in Viet Nam, he had never, not put his ship down, no matter how hot the LZ (landing zone) was. Mays once landed his ship, loaded with wounded, with a tail rotor that spun off upon landing and its windshield shot out. He'd never been afraid – it was only in his dreams that he was a coward. *Like some FNG* (Fucking New Guy). His idiosyncrasy was to curse his way down and, then, again up. Mays said that it chased away his fear. Because he was being broadcasted, he was known for this, as well as for his heroics.

I don't blame Diane for leaving me, she endured this shit for fifteen years – longer than I spent in-country(Vietnam) thought Mays. *I had the best; she was too good for me. I miss her so much.*

He then bawled like a baby – not *in* a dream, but *of* a dream that had been shattered.

❧ Chapter Fifty-Seven ❧

Tito looked over at the directions lying on the passenger seat, on how to navigate through the residential area; houses with both garages for cars, and hangers for airplanes, and then over to the Airpark. A sign led him to the airport runway, and as Mays had said, he found rows of airplane hangers. He drove slowly past three hangers, before he saw Coleman Mays. Or at least it looked like it might be him, a black man about the same age as his father. Tito pulled his car up to a split rail fence, and along side a vintage Porsche.

"Coleman Mays?" Tito called out.

"That would be me." Mays answered.

Tito walked over to him. He was smaller than his father had described. *Or maybe it was the stories that were told which made him a larger than life person.*

"Glad to meet you Senior Lopez." Mays extended his hand.

"Tito Lopez," said Tito, as he took Mays' hand. "Growing up in my house, you were a legend," added Tito.

"Don't believe all that stuff. Ordinary lives can grow into

legends – depending on the storyteller. In *my* house I was definitely *not* a legend."

"My dad was the storyteller and he is the most truthful, honest man I know."

"Can't argue with you there Tito," said Mays.

Mays opened the automatic overhead hanger door. "Give me a hand in pulling my baby out."

Mays explained that it was a Cessna *Skyhawk.* "It's not new, but it's mine – no bank."

"It's beautiful, and I like the color, blue, with blue pin stripping," said Tito.

"You'll like her up in the air too. Ever been up in a small plane?"

"No."

"Well you're in for a treat; it'll help take your mind off of the mission. In fact if you ever thought about buying a boat, after this experience, you might be changing your mind."

Mays proceeded to go through an extensive check list. Check if there's water in the fuel, check oil, check for bird nests, prop, tires, etc.

"Can't be too careful, there isn't a breakdown lane up there."

"Can I ask you a favor?" Tito asked.

"Sure, lay it on me."

"I'd like to put my car in the hanger, if that's possible."

"Sure, no problem," said Mays.

They slipped the rails out of the fence and Tito drove his car into the hanger.

"I take it that someone is following you?"

"You *could* say that. I used some diversionary tactics by first going over to Hyannis, before coming here. I think

I lost him at the Hyannis Airport, but he's probably figured it out by now."

Mays took two rifle cases from the Porsche.

"Is that an M-16?" asked Tito, in a joking way.

"Not exactly," said Mays.

Now Tito wasn't so sure of the joke.

Mays put them into the compartment behind the back seat and looked at Tito for his contribution.

"It's okay, Cole, you don't mind if I call you Cole? I'm carrying mine."

"No problem with Cole, I've been called worse." His thoughts went to his ex-wife.

They got into the cabin and taxied over to the self-service fuel depot. Mays cut the engine and proceeded to fill the fuel tanks. He gave Tito head phones to wear.

"I feel like a counterfeit pilot with these on." He looked over at Mays and it was a different story. Mays looked confident and looked the part.

"Nothing like it, man. I should have made a career of the military and stayed off the ground. It's the terra firma that I had trouble with. Instead I got out, took a job in engineering, made money, and fucked up my marriage. If I stayed in, I would have been happy flying and maybe brought some of that happiness home. My job made me miserable, the guys I worked with didn't have a clue of what it was like in Nam. I came home from the job, pissed off at them and unable to shake the ghosts. I needed help, but I found out too late. So am I doing Hector a favor? No, he's doing me a favor. This is the best I've felt in a long time."

Tito didn't say anything back. He could see how the

love his father felt for his mother helped to keep away the demons of war.

"I have the transponder shut off. We won't be able to avoid *all* controlled air space, but we'll do the best we can," said Mays.

The Cessna taxied to the end of the runway and turned around. Mays looked at Tito, winked, and said, "*Vamonos!*"

The engine roared as they barreled down the runway, going airborne, they banked to the right.

"Sit back and enjoy the scenery. The stewardess will be by to tend to your needs. Our first stop will be in Pennsylvania. There isn't any tower there. We'll fly in unannounced, and re-fuel." Mays proclaimed.

∽

Cape Cod, Massachusetts/Amarillo, Texas

"I'm at the Airpark, it looks deserted – no one is even at the fuel pump," said the Agent.

"Keep looking around, what else is there?" asked Tolson.

"There are rows of big attached buildings with roll up doors. Those are probably hangers. I see a Porsche parked at one of the rows."

"That's it! There is a Porsche registered to Mays. Check it out."

"I'm out looking at it now. Hey, there are tire tracks going under the split rail fence. They lead to one of the hangers."

"Break in!" shouted Tolson.

The Agent read off the license plate number of Tito's car, and Tolson quickly traced it to the NYPD.

Tolson called Parsons.

"We know they're together and in the air," said Tolson.

"I'll get the right people working this. Lopez and the girl are in Amarillo, and now we have a GPS in the form of an airplane, leading us to them. Have your men ready, only use *Apostles*. We're about to get rid of a couple of gnats. Don't spare the armament and you don't have to clean up after you. Leave them there and let them bleed out."

❧ CHAPTER FIFTY-EIGHT ❧

The flight, over mountainous terrain to State College, Pennsylvania took 3 hours and 26 minutes. Cole taxied the plane over to the fueling station and repeated the same process he did at the Falmouth Airpark. Tito got out and stretched his legs.

"We're going to fly out at six thousand feet; we got enough fuel for five hours." Mays said.

Tito nodded his head. "I have no idea what that all means, but I trust you do, and that's good enough for me. If it wasn't for the nature of the trip, I might even find it enjoyable. But, that said, I'm worried for my brother."

This time is was Mays who nodded his head.

He checked the plane, again, going through all of the safety procedures. It passed his inspection and they were once again airborne.

During the flight, Tito, for want of something to do, checked his 9mm. He laughed as he imagined doing this on a regular commercial flight. He let Mays in on his thought, which drew a chuckle.

"How are you doing?" Tito asked Mays.

"I'm fine, but we'll be resting in Indiana."

Four hours and ten minutes later, with a howling wind coming out of the South, they landed on runway eighteen with just two hundred feet to spare.

"Welcome to Sky King Airport," said Mays

"Wasn't he a super hero from the forties and fifties?" Tito asked.

"I think he was a comic book hero, but don't quote me." answered Mays

Their supper came from the airport's vending machines.

"We'll rest here and take off at the crack of dawn – I'm qualified, but I'm not much for flying at night." They reclined their seats.

∽

Amarillo, Texas/Washington, D.C.

Tolson's cell phone cracked with the sound of Parsons voice.

"They just landed in Indiana. We're following their flight and we'll get all of them when they reach Amarillo."

"Yes sir, that's great news. I'm ready to move out with my men; as you requested, all of them are *Apostles*."

❧ Chapter Fifty-Nine ❧

Alexandria, Virginia

The long driveway could accommodate over fifty cars, but tonight, cars had to park out on the road.

"I've called all of you here, because our goal is about to be realized. Tomorrow, General Thompson will be leaving Fort Bragg with five thousand men – a brigade. Our other 'Apostle' Generals will be on alert, to march, if necessary. I, for one, don't think it will be necessary. The President will be removed, Senator Parsons will be installed, and the *Apostles* will reign over all."

The applause was deafening - from the Great Room and from the overflow crowd in the adjacent rooms.

Alastair Watts was proud of this moment, a time that he knew *would* come. He had topped Forbes' "richest man in the world" list for so long now, that no one could name the person in second place. His house, this night, was filled with other important businessmen, politicians, judges, and dignitaries representing all of the major religions.

"Tomorrow," Watts continued, "Senator Parsons," he gestured to Parsons who was standing next to him, "will announce a massive tax cut, which should bring more of our countryman to our way of thinking. We are going to pull back our military from all over the world, eliminate all foreign aid and all charitable support. Senator Parsons will be announcing this, and more."

There was more thunderous applause, this time Watts needed to raise his hand to quell it.

He nodded and smiled at Parsons, who acknowledged him back.

"Until we are sure of a victory, we'll hold off on your Presidency."

Parsons nodded again, and thought; *now we know who the real President is.*

Watts continued, "We are not going to make the same mistakes that Hitler made, but we *will* control everything. Not that we don't already."

Laughter filled the room with a few high fives.

"The spoils belong to the privileged, and rightly so. We're smarter, we've had money for a longer time, therefore, we know best what to do with it; and now we're going to get more of it."

Applause and laughter followed.

"The mistake that Hitler made was that he was not all-inclusive. The *Apostles* will be the new religion. We will come out of the shadows and let *everyone* sign on. Of course being a member of a party doesn't mean all will be treated equally. It never has. The new members will be *Apostles* in name only. We, here, and a few that could not make it, are the elite, and will be treated as thus. There is much work to do, and more time then we have to cover it, so I will now take questions."

A voice came from the back, "What about the Second Amendment?"

"It's dead and we're going to leave it that way, after all we had nothing to do with eliminating it," said Watts. "We will allow ownership of guns on a select basis, without bringing on the spectacle of the Second Amendment."

"Do we have a roll for the military?" said a voice up front.

"My answer to that is, since we'll no longer serve as the policemen of the world, we will cut our military across the board. Our emphasis will be on modern weaponry. We will strive to have all members of the military, not just the generals, be members of the *Apostles*. In other words we'll have home grown mercenaries. Patriotism, which is on the wane anyway, will be discouraged, Unions will be outlawed, and loyalty to the *Apostles* will become the new order. We will solve world problems monetarily. And our negotiations will be with the world's financial leaders, not with their elected, appointed, or 'ascended to the throne,' frauds. These are the moves that will cut our taxes. The majority should see a five hundred dollar tax benefit, we of course, being in the highest tax brackets will reap tens of thousands of dollars. I hope that I have answered most of your important concerns. The bars are open and the caterers will be moving among you."

There was final applause.

❧ CHAPTER SIXTY ❧

Thursday: A.M./P.M.

Tito watched the necessary repetition of Mays' safety ritual. *It was working, the plane was behaving, and now they we're almost there.*

At 7 a.m. they took off from Terre Haute and 3 hours and ten minutes later, landed at a small airfield in Springfield, Missouri. Tito never left the plane. Mays, again, did his refueling routine, and they were off to Amarillo, Texas. Tito had a restless night's sleep and was half awake when Mays mentioned the name of the Springfield airport. *It sounded like a cowboy ranch*, thought Tito. He tried to be interested, but his thoughts were only of Danny and Kristen.

"When we get close to the Palo Duro Airport, in Texas, we're going to veer off and head south to the pick-up point," said Mays. "And when we get within ten minutes of landing, you call Danny and give him the location. Whoever is tracking us will be able to pick up the broadcast, but I'm figuring they're about sixty minutes away from the time we alert Danny, so we have fifty minutes to play with."

"Gotcha," said Tito. "How much time do we have to go?"

"We have a little over four hours before it's crunch time," said Mays.

"Since we're being tracked, what plan, if any, do you have to avoid them *after* we pick up Danny and Kristen?" Tito asked.

"Good question," said Mays. "We're going to fly at tree top level and land on a private air strip that a friend of mine has on his property. He and I are in a Vietnam Veteran's flying club, and although he doesn't know it yet, he's going to lend us one of his antique planes. Let's just say that I'm calling in my markers on an old debt that *he* thinks he owes me."

"I envy you and my Dad for the fraternity you have, even though it was earned in hell."

"It was the hell that we shared, that makes us give back to our brothers who were there. This fraternity is built on pain and anguish. No one who wasn't actually there could ever understand. It was tough when we returned, everyone else was running around in la la land, laughing and carrying on as if nothing had happened. Something *was* happening, and when you tried to explain that we had just returned from defending their freedom, they looked at you as if, somehow, we soldiers had provoked and caused the war. It pissed me off, and only caused me to go deeper within myself. It wasn't like it is now, with Iraq, the carnage then, was buried between baseball scores, 'Mets 6 and Pittsburgh 5, *Fifty-seven were killed today in Vietnam*, St. Louis 8, Philadelphia 5.'" Mays' voice trailed off. Tito didn't respond and the cockpit became quiet.

The silence was broken by Mays, "Wake up Tito! Call your brother"

∽

Danny had already packed the rental car as his cell phone blurted out the Valkyrie theme.

"What is it Danny?" asked Kristen.

"Tito is in the air, and is about ten minutes from here."

"Where are we going?" Kristen asked.

"To a crop dusting field called, 'Cally's Spraying Airport.'"

❧ CHAPTER SIXTY-ONE ❧

Thursday: A.M.

A perfectly preserved 1955 Jeep was the first vehicle out of Fort Bragg. It was 9 a.m., and there were people already lined up to cheer the troop's departure. Signs of 'Parsons for President' were spattered among the turnout.

Major General Spencer Thompson waved to the crowd, as he led a brigade of 5,000 men out of the front gate. The way to the White House would normally take about six hours, but with the caravan, and the Thursday commuter traffic, the troops would not get there until 7 p.m.

Chief of Staff Aaron Herzog was motioned into the oval office by President Dominic Forcelli. Forcelli raised his hand, before Herzog could speak.

"I know, I've seen him on T.V., the pompous ass. The only thing that he's missing is the pipe and the sunglasses. And when he gets here, I'll fire him just like Truman did to *his* general."

"Mr. President, our situation may be a bit more serious than what Truman faced."

"Aaron, how many times have I told you, that when we're alone, please use my first name. We grew up in the same housing project in The Bronx, and have known each other our entire lives, for crying out loud."

"Okay, Mr. President," said Herzog, with a smile.

Claire Dempsey poked her head into the Oval Office. "Mr. President, I have the Chairman of the Joint Chiefs Of Staff, Admiral Benoit, on line number one."

Forcelli answered, "Yes, Joseph, I believe I know what you're calling about."

"Mr. President, you and I don't agree on many things, but we both believe that our country, and the Constitution it is governed by, is the best there is. I can have an army intercept General Thompson before he gets to the White House."

"I appreciate your support, Joe, but what I don't want is our country to be a mirror image of Rome. God knows, since my Presidency, I've heard more than once, my term being compared to the 'Fall of Rome.' I don't want opposing armies marching on Washington. I have confidence in the American people, that they will not let this happen."

"You and I have seen what the American people are capable of, and how they favor words over service, specifically, yours and mine," said Benoit.

"This is true, and I have depended on that service to be our common denominator. Because of it, I trust you, and I trust that you will be at my side, if and when I need you."

"You can depend upon me, Mr. President," said Benoit.

"Thank you, Joe."

As the phone was hung up, Claire Dempsey poked her head, again, into the Oval Office.

"What now, Claire? A war has been declared? Pestilence has arrived? If it's pestilence, you may be correct, it's *about* to arrive." Forcelli quipped.

"I have a group of men in the main conference room, who would like to speak to you," said Claire Dempsey.

"You're kidding, right? How did they get past all the red tape leading up to the Oval Office?"

"When you see them, you'll know why," she said.

"Claire, is everybody loosing their minds around me? We've got a crisis on our hands. This is not the time for sightseers."

"Mr. President, please look through the doorway to the conference room. They are not sightseers, they're here to help."

Forcelli's curiosity took over, mostly because his secretary was 'by the book,' and had never been *pushy*. Forcelli followed her to the conference room and peeked in.

"My God! My God!" He exclaimed.

Forcelli backed off and returned to the Oval Office.

"Bring them in here, Claire, and Aaron, please stay."

❦ Chapter Sixty-Two ❦

Thursday: P.M.

Tolson's phone rang.

"Yes sir!"

"They're going to an airfield south of Amarillo called 'Cally's Spraying Airport.' We have to believe that Lopez is closer than you are. I'm sure he was set up in that way. You know what you have to do," said Parsons.

"Yes sir, we're leaving right now," said Tolson

Mays positioned the Cessna in line with the dirt runway.

"It looks deserted. I got a feeling that Cally's Airport has seen better days. We're going in, brace yourself in case we hit a divot," said Mays.

The landing was not smooth.

"Man they got some nerve in calling this an airport."

After the final bounce, the plane rolled over smooth surface and came to a halt.

"Where'd that come from?" said Mays referring to the level dirt. "This place has been abandoned for a long time.

Fortunately I didn't expect to fuel up here; we have enough to get to my friend's place."

As they taxied around, Tito noted a road entering from where they would be taking off.

"What does the temperature say, Cole?"

"It says 107 degrees." Man, I don't want to stay here any longer then it takes to get your brother out."

"I see a vehicle coming from up the road," said Tito. He got out of the plane to both, greet them, and show them a friendly face.

"Tito!" Danny called out. Danny and Kristen had condensed their belongings down to one medium size suite case and one small carry bag. The rest of what was taken for the trip was placed into a 'Goodwill' bin. Danny took the suite case from the trunk; Kristen was right behind him with her carry bag. As they were gathering their belongings, Tito spoke to Mays through the open cockpit door, "It's good to see that my brother and his girlfriend are safe."

"That white dude is your brother?" asked Mays.

"That would be him," said Tito.

"Your father is something else, he never changed. I hope you know that you're blessed."

"I know that, Cole, but thanks for reminding me."

Tito opened the area behind the back seat and slid the suitcase in. Kristen handed Tito her bag, and that too was placed into storage.

"Cole, this is Kristen and my brother Danny."

Cole extended his hand to Danny and Kristen, noting to himself, how slender Kristen's hand was, and how it compared to his ex-wife.

"Okay, everybody seat belted?"

All answered yes.

"Then we are cleared for take-off. I'm trying to make this as professional as possible."

Mays pushed the throttle forward and the Cessna started down the runway.

Tito felt the difference from the other take-offs. Something was not right. Immediately, Cole announced, "It won't lift off!"

The plane went beyond the runway, and onto the hardscrabble terrain.

Before anyone could ask, Cole said, "We got a problem. Could be the heat, could be the goddamn southwest desert, or it could be we have too much weight. I think it was the heat, so we'll try it again."

"What's that?" asked Danny. He was looking out the back of the plane, and at the glaring sun bouncing off of three vehicles coming down the only road in. They were almost at the spot where Danny and Kristen had boarded the plane.

"We can't take the plane back up the runway, which means we can't take off," said Mays. He looked around and decided. "The plane stays here, we go. Okay, everybody out of the plane! Tito, hand me my rifle cases. You take this one, leave it in its case, for now, it's a semi-automatic rifle, and the ammo and clips are in the bag. I'm going to divert their attention by running over to that beat up shed. You, Danny and Kristen, are to get yourselves to those rocks and scruffy looking bushes; leave the bags in the plane." He took his rifle from its case.

"Is that an M14?" asked Tito.

"Not exactly, it's kind of an M14, but without fully automatic firing. Okay, are we all set?"

Three heads nodded.

"Then let's go!"

Tito, Danny and Kristen left first, and on a dead run, headed over to the mini oasis. The three cars had entered the runway and were coming fast. As shots were fired from the speeding vehicles, at the trio, Mays left his position at the plane.

He leveled his weapon at his hip and began firing at the oncoming cars. He kept firing – *I have fifty feet to go*, he thought. Mays saw that his passengers had made it to the rocks. All of the attention was on him as he continued to fire and replace ammo clips. He was hitting his targets, and the return fire was intense. He needed to go ten more feet to reach the shed. In Vietnam his wounds were not physical; they were the kind where Purple Hearts were not awarded. But now he was hit and then hit again and again. His weapon grew silent. Mays would not be receiving a Purple Heart, here, either.

"I think Mays is dead," said Kristen.

"I think you're right," said Tito. "We have a rifle and my 9mm." Danny held up his revolver. "And a revolver." Tito added.

The Agents had not yet taken their attention off of Mays.

Without saying a word, Kristen used Muldoon's cell phone, with its New Mexico number (to be displayed), and dialed 911.

Danny's eyes widened with surprise, as Kristen, using

a thick Texan drawl, began to explain to the operator, her difficult situation.

"I'm here with my husband," she said slowly, "and we had to make an emergency landing at Cally's Airport," her voice rose, "when all of a sudden there were these terrorists screaming that they were CIA agents, but I *know* that they weren't." Kristen paused and sobbed. "They killed our pilot. I know they aren't real, real patriots wouldn't do that. And they're not from around here either, they have *New York accents*," she emphasized.

"Maam, don't you worry. *Our* law enforcement doesn't work like that. You and your husband, y'all keep your heads down, we'll be right at your service."

"That was amazing," said Danny.

"I'm assuming they're coming?" asked Tito.

"Yes they are." Kristen answered. "I told you that I would be useful."

"Okay, here is what we do. If they're not already shooting at us, when the cavalry arrives, we will fire at them in order to get them to fire back, and look like the aggressors they are," said Tito.

"Looks like we got one of them, now let's take the rest of them out," said Tolson.

Their automatic weapons concentrated on the trio's position and the shells were chipping away at the rocks.

Danny asked Tito, "What did you say about coaxing them to fire at us?"

The onslaught was so intense, that they could not put their heads up to return fire. When there was a short lull, they managed to get a few rounds in, but soon again, the barrage continued.

They heard and felt the change. Rounds were being fired that were not making contact with the rocks. Tito looked up and saw a fierce fire fight going on. There were at least ten marked cars that, based on Kristen's call, were shooting at first sight.

❧ CHAPTER SIXTY-THREE ❧

Thursday: P.M.

The going was slow. The convoy was impeded by its size, the normal commuter traffic, two small fender benders, and now, just outside of Richmond, a major accident with fatalities. The operation was at a standstill.

"My estimate of 7 p.m. looks like it was right on target," said Thompson.

"Yes sir, it certainly does," answered Captain Kovin. Kovin was Thompson's aide, and never voiced a contrary word. When he was asked for his opinion, he knew what Thompson wanted, and that was the opinion he gave.

"I'm getting hungry, what do you say we pull out of this mess and get some lunch?" Thompson's statement was more of an order than a question.

"That sounds like a good idea, sir," said Captain Kovin, being true to his word.

"Sergeant Crocker! Take the next exit off," Kovin ordered.

"Get me Gleeson on the phone," said Thompson.

Colonel Philip Gleeson was Thompson's Chief of Staff

and was in the vehicle behind Thompson's Jeep. He was not yet an *Apostle*.

"Phil, I'll catch up with you at the White House. You'll be taking in the main contingent, and I should be getting there at about the same time." said Thompson.

"Understood," said Gleeson.

Sergeant Crocker took the next exit off of I-95.

"I know a great place, not far from here, Kasani's Restaurant," said Kovin.

"Is that an Italian name?" asked Thompson.

"It's an Italian Restaurant, but that's not an Italian name. There are no K's in the Italian language," said Kovin. They use two c's to make a 'k' sound."

"Hmmm that's interesting. There was a time when the *guineas* ruled the underworld. After today, with the *Apostles* in charge, there will be no underworld, not the Asians, not the Russians, no one. The *Apostles* will be able to deal with all insurgents of that type, as they should have been dealt with, long ago. Our judicial system will be streamlined and our executions will be devoid of red tape. Our society, with the *Apostles* as its foundation, will become a beacon for other countries to follow. Our loyalty and patriotism will be to the *Apostles*. Freedom as it exists today, went too far, and included too many people. Our tax system became too liberal; Parsons will put us on the right track."

After dinner, which included more speeches by Thompson, they were on the road again, and at 6:30 p.m. they were thirty minutes from the Capitol.

At 7:05 p.m. Major General Spencer Thompson arrived at the White House. He expected Colonel Gleeson, to have already, secured, and entered the building. The next step was to remove President Forcelli and escort Parsons, from his Senate office, and into the White House. Thompson relished the thought of personally doing it. Instead, as Thompson strode up to the front of his troops, he was met by Gleeson.

"Is everything going as planned?" asked Thompson.

"No sir, I'm sorry to report that we hit a snag. Our men refuse to cross the line and enter the White House, and frankly, I.....well you will see," replied Gleeson.

"WHAT THE FUCK ARE YOU TALKING ABOUT? WHAT FUCKING LINE?"

Thompson, with Gleeson in tow, pushed his way past his troops. As he got closer to the front the soldiers thinned out, until he came to a clearing and the entrance to the White House. He was taken back at the sight.

"What the ....?"

Standing in solemn, 'parade rest,' their hands clasped behind them, twenty men stood proud. Some wore fatigues with their name on them, others wore remnants of uniforms, and others wore civilian clothes. But the one thing in common that they all wore, was, The Congressional Medal Of Honor around their necks. In the center was Hector Lopez.

Thompson turned to one of the soldiers, "Corporal! Take your weapon and make a path through those insurgents."

"That would not be a wise idea, General." said President Forcelli.

Forcelli, with his ever present cane, had stepped out from behind Hector Lopez, and became the twenty-first wearer of The Congressional Medal Of Honor.

"General Thompson," Forcelli stated. "You are not only fired, but these men, Special Agent Monteiro of the FBI,

Agent O'Connor of the CIA and Chief of Police Martel Evans of the D.C. Police, are here, jointly, to arrest you for treasonous acts against the United States Government. Chief of Police Evans, you may read him his rights."

Forcelli turned to Gleeson, "Colonel, Gleeson is it?" He read off of his name tag.

"Yes sir, Mr. President," he answered.

"I want you to take these men back to Bragg, tonight. I don't need anymore traffic jams and I will see to it that, you, and your men, will not be held responsible for what went on here today."

"Thank you, Mr. President," said Gleeson as he saluted. Forcelli saluted back.

ॐ

Parsons looked up from his desk at the two men who had just entered his office.

"I thought that General Thompson would be doing the honors?" said Parsons.

"Actually the honor is ours," said Special Agent Monteiro. "Agent O'Connor and I are here to place you under arrest. The charges are serious, voting manipulation in Congress, murder in the first degree, and not the least of all, treason. Your aide, Mr. Mann, has already been arrested."

"I…I don't understand," said Parsons.

"That's right," said Monteiro. "You didn't get it. You underestimated the patriotism that runs deep within us. A feeling that transcends political parties, a feeling that I guess, you don't have."

A third man entered the office.

"This is Chief of Police Evans; he'll read you your rights – something that you were trying to get rid of."

∾

The next morning, Forcelli, fulfilled a promise he made to Hector. He personally called the Governor of Texas to obtain the release of Danny, Kristen and Tito; arrested for weapons violations, after the shootout, which killed Tolson and all of his men.

❧ CHAPTER SIXTY-FOUR ❧

Following Two Years

As their numbers shrunk, and their ulterior motives were understood, the Apostle movement all but disappeared. Because of the tactics employed by the Apostles, President Forcelli had a change of heart. He carried the torch for restoring the Second Amendment, and took it a step further, noting, "how the birth of our country was different than that of Europe, and the rest of the world," he campaigned for a uniform licensing by the states, of all firearms, and with it, a national right to carry reciprocity across state lines; no different than the acceptance of state driver's licenses. "Just because it was written at our infancy, it is in no way irrelevant or obsolete. It is part of our freedoms, and defense of our freedoms from any source, internal or external," wrote Forcelli. He enjoyed a renewed respect, congress worked together for the common good; projects were passed on their merit and not politicized. Forcelli was overwhelmingly re-elected for a second term.

∽

Danny and Kristen were married within six months. The entire Lopez family, along with Senator Marchand and Richard Steinitz, were flown, at Marchand's expense, to Candelaria, New Mexico. Bishop Shamus Muldoon performed the wedding ceremony in Saint Michael's Church. The day before the wedding, at an overflowing mass, Danny gave the homily.

∾

Before the year was out, President Forcelli, recognized the heroic effort that Hector undertook, by awarding him The Medal of Freedom. "In defending, once again, the country that he loves, and for his contribution and meritorious conduct in preserving the security of our nation," stated Forcelli.

Another Medal of Freedom was awarded posthumously to Coleman Mays. Mays' ex-wife accepted the award.

∾

Alastair Watts, facing charges of complicity in attempting to overthrow the United States Government, fled to Switzerland where he was granted asylum. He is still the wealthiest man in the world.

∾

A senate enquiry into the assassination of President John F. Kennedy was being spearheaded by Senator Charles Marchand, using additional evidence gathered from anonymous sources.

❧ ABOUT THE AUTHOR ❧

Tom Salvador formerly of Long Island, New York, now resides with his family on Cape Cod, Massachusetts. He is a professional musician, has a B.S. degree in Accounting, and is an army veteran.